Lillington, Kenneth. An ash-blonde witch.
Mar. 1987. [138p.] Faber & Faber; dist. by
Harper, $10.95 (0-571-14325-2). Galley.

Lillington, who has a knack for tempering real-
ity with a misty overlay of the supernatural,
takes a slight detour from his regular route in a
charming, funny, hectic novel, in which a
young woman of the twenty-second century
wreaks havoc among the blissfully ignorant
peasants of Urstwhile, a village carefully pre-
served from days of yore. Characters are wonderful. There is resident wicked witch, Dorcas,
"a real professional" whose "nose and chin
met"; stalwart, chivalrous Simon, the farmer,
whose inexperience with the fair sex becomes
painfully obvious when two women fall in love
with him simultaneously; prudish Prudence,
self-proclaimed judge of Urstwhile morals; and
finally lovely blonde Sophie, a stranger from
beyond the mountains, whose acquaintance
with autosuggestion and hypnotism makes her
not only Dorcas' rival but also a serious con-
tender for Prudence's wrath. Superstition and
science meld delightfully with one another and
with the makings of simple romance as this
strange assortment of people are thrown together to escape villagers bent on purging
Urstwhile of its witchy goings-on. Gr. 9–12.
SZ. *BKL - 1/15/87*

AN ASH-BLONDE WITCH

ff

AN
ASH-BLONDE
WITCH

Kenneth
Lillington

faber and faber
LONDON · BOSTON

First published in 1987
by Faber and Faber Limited
3 Queen Square London WC1N 3AU

Typeset by Goodfellow & Egan, Cambridge
Printed in Great Britain by
Redwood Burn Ltd, Trowbridge, Wiltshire

British Library Cataloguing in Publication Data

Lillington, Kenneth
An ash-blonde witch.
I. Title
823'.914 [J]   PZ7

ISBN 0-571-14625-2

For Sophie Margaret Lynch

An Ash-blonde Witch

Ash, of course, is not blonde. That was just some poet trying to be clever. Her hair in fact was pale gold, unlike the mousy thatch of most of the natives, and quite lovely enough to set poets hunting for words.

The rumours about her were absurd. It was said that on the night of her arrival she had sheltered in a farmhouse during a storm, and that in spite of the rain her clothes had been quite dry; but no-one knew which farmhouse nor who owned it. It was said that the pupils of her eyes, which were of such startling blue that no-one could look in them, were not round, but vertical slits, like a cat's.

She and her father had taken a small cottage one mile south of the town. He puzzled everyone too. It was said that he was doing 'research'. 'Research'? It had something to do with sitting indoors and writing. And *that* was how he earned his living?

Father and daughter spoke the language fluently, but they were certainly not natives of the tiny valley kingdom of Urstwile. They must have come from beyond the great mountain ridge that cut that kingdom off from the rest of the world. Yet many quite intelligent Urstwileans doubted whether there was life beyond the mountains, and children were sometimes told that that region was the abode of devils.

The father seldom showed his face. The daughter came into town almost daily. Heads were turned wherever she went. She conducted herself very properly, but she had a secret air of total self-assurance, and of course she was very beautiful. Her dress was modest, but her supple curves made it seem to glitter as she walked. Once a poet, as she passed him, was overheard to sigh, 'O how that glittering taketh me!' and was fined on the spot.

The manners of the men of Urstwile were very good, but she deranged them. They all seemed to think that she needed protection, and positively elbowed one another in the face to give it her. They rushed to open doors for her, to hold parcels for her, and to help her over kerbs. One fool even threw his cloak into a puddle for her to step on, quite needlessly, because she changed direction at that moment and didn't even see him.

The result was that wives fell out with their husbands.

Prudence, the tax collector's daughter, was even more censorious than the other women. The new girl's allure, she felt, could only lead to immorality. Prudence, although only seventeen, already regarded herself as a judge of the community's morals. She condemned all public displays of affection, and if she found courting couples canoodling in doorways or on the park benches, she would give them a piece of her mind. Truth to tell, she disapproved of sex altogether. She thought that God ought to have devised a nicer way for people to be born, yet she was reluctant to criticise God, because in the main she thought very highly of Him. She was destined to become a priestess.

Destiny she was sure it was. Simon, the handsome young farmer, once asked her, with his usual courtesy, whether she didn't ever want any other kind of job. 'Ah,' Prudence replied, 'it's not what we want, it's what God wants, isn't it?' He felt that she'd snubbed him, somehow.

The community harboured one member already who was certainly a witch – the hag Dorcas, who lived in a hovel in Cankered Wood off the north end of the town. She was a real professional. She wore a pointed hat and a cloak sewn over with strange symbols. Her nose and chin met. Her companion was a great black cat whose eyes curved like scimitars. She could raise storms and give you toothache, and if you visited her and she took a dislike to you, she could shuffle the trees around. Rumour had it that there were some who had never found their way out again, and could be heard at night roaming the wood and filling it with their tragic cries.

Prudence thought it disgraceful that Dorcas should be allowed to live and thrive. She wanted her dragged into the town on a hurdle, ducked in the park lake, and then burned in the market place – after a proper trial, of course, the result of which however would be a fore-gone conclusion. Prudence wanted all this so earnestly because she was very religious and good. She went to the town elders and begged them to do something about it. At least, she pleaded, Dorcas should be stood in the pillory. The elders smiled at her pretty enthusiasm, but they didn't act.

The fact was, they judged it wise to turn a blind eye, because Dorcas had friends in high places, including several enchanted princesses and a baron or two. Let's face it, they confided in one another, a woman like that made life safer for her middle-class sisters. Her presence was really quite healthy. It was an open secret that one

3

or two of them visited her themselves, in quest of lucky charms, or spells to use against enemies, or simply potions to rejuvenate their own failing powers.

Prudence came down the steps of the Council Chamber in a rage.

'All right,' she muttered, as she stood on the pavement, 'just let her come into town when it's raining!'

'Why?' enquired a passing matron.

'Leave footprints, won't she?'

'I suppose we all will.'

'You'll see.'

A day or two later, it did rain, and Dorcas, who preferred foul weather to fine on principle, did come into town in her pointed hat and her black cloak with its yellow symbols; and Prudence, gibbering under her breath, followed her at a distance, carrying a hammer and a bag of nails.

Eventually the hag entered a shop in front of which some wooden boards had been placed to cover the puddles, and Prudence, flushed and panting a little, waited alongside until she came out again. Dorcas gave her a brief glare of her yellow eyes, but Prudence was already sticking out two fingers of her left hand, like a prong, to ward off evil, and Dorcas cackled shortly and made off. She had indeed left a footprint, and Prudence, heedless of muddying her dress, knelt beside it, her hair falling about her face, and began banging a nail into it.

A small group of women gathered round.

'Shouldn't meddle with her, Prudence,' said one.

'I shall *force* them to acknowledge that she's a witch,' panted Prudence.

'Eveyone knows that.'

'I shall bring it into the light.'

'I wouldn't cross her for love or money.'

If you drove a nail into a witch's footprint, she would be fixed to the spot, wherever she happened to be. In theory, that was. The women looked to where Dorcas was scuttling away. It didn't seem to be working.

'Just you watch!' gasped Prudence. The exertion was making her hot, sweaty, and most uncomely. The rain made rats' tails of her hair. Two nails buckled up before they were half in. She wrenched them out furiously with the claw side of the hammer, and started on a third. This one she did drive home.

'Now!' she cried, and gave the nail a final blow.

The head of the hammer stuck to the nail, and the haft of the hammer stuck to Prudence.

'Oh dear,' said the women.

'She has put a spell on me,' said Prudence, choking.

'Afraid so, dear.'

'*Help* me, then!'

'Oh no,' said the women. 'We are not meddling with her!'

'You can't leave me like this!'

'Perhaps the spell will wear off.'

'I'm getting soaked!'

'Yes,' agreed the women, who were all good motherly souls, 'we can't just leave her. Should we tell the Council?'

'They will take note of your communication, and start thinking about it in three months' time,' said one.

'True. There's Simon. He may help.'

The handsome young farmer, who had joined the crowd, was led forward. He knelt beside Prudence and took her thin arm in his huge hands, to which the plough and the scythe had given a mighty grip.

'Don't take advantage of me, now,' snapped Prudence.

'No fear of that, lass,' said Simon soothingly, and

pulled gently on her forearm. Women he regarded as delicate and unpredictable creatures.

He was sorry for Prudence, not just at present, but in general, because it was in his nature to sympathise with the unloved. For Prudence, for all her goodness, was unloved. She had been so right from her school-days, when the teacher used to depute her to take the names of those who were talking or running in the corridor. Simon was probably the only person who had a soft spot for her on this very account. It was sad, he felt, to be born with a nature like hers. You couldn't choose your own nature, so if you had a nice one you could count yourself lucky and not be smug about it.

He pulled more strongly. It was as if he were trying to lift the whole earth. He gripped the head of the hammer itself, so as not to hurt the girl's arm, brought his foot into play, and heaved. The hammer remained welded to the ground. He let go and wiped his brow.

'We might saw the haft in two,' he suggested.

'And leave me clutching the half of it for the rest of my life?'

A new voice was heard among the crowd.

'What are you up to? Stop tormenting the poor girl!'

It was the blonde stranger, sharp and indignant, pushing her way imperiously to the fore. The women growled resentfully. They did not think of her as a witch as yet, but she had already antagonised them.

'We're not tormenting her, we're trying to help her, and see if you can do better, if you're so clever!'

'Uppity little madam.'

'Kid half our age.'

She ignored them and went up to Simon, raising her starry blue eyes to him. He blinked as though she had flashed a mirror in his face.

'What is her name?'

6

'Prudence, Miss.'

'Prudence. What are you up to, Prudence?'

'The witch Dorcas has put a spell on her,' said the women.

Quietly and respectfully, Simon explained. The girl kept her eyes on him, shaking her head in wonder, finding this tale beyond belief. 'I see,' she said, but stopped and shook her head, as if words had failed her. 'Well! We'd better take it off her, hadn't we?'

Prudence, soaking, bedraggled, and humiliated, glared up at her. She squatted, looking Prudence in the eyes, and Prudence's sulky look changed to one of rising fear. 'Come along now, Prudence,' she said, in a quiet voice full of authority, 'let go the hammer and stand up.'

Prudence let go the hammer and stood up. The girl picked up the hammer and handed it to her.

'Now if I were you, I should go home and change.'

For a moment Prudence looked as if she were about to bring the hammer down on the new girl's head, but then without a word she stumbled shamefacedly away.

'Auto-suggestion,' murmured the girl, as if marvelling to herself. 'Fascinating.'

Her strange words, half-heard, not at all understood, awed the crowd. They parted for her as she walked away.

Her name, they learned, was Sophie Margaret Oakroyd. They were rather disappointed, because by now the rumours were in spate, and they had expected something more exotic, like Morveena or Zillia or even Morgan le Fay. Sophie went about innocent of her new reputation.

It was soon to be enhanced.

Reuben, the town blacksmith, had toothache. He was

like a great baby, roaring and lashing about. His wife was in despair because he had already smashed up the furniture in his frenzy, and given her a few contusions and abrasions in the course of doing so. She had called a local tooth-drawer in, but when the forceps had approached Reuben's mouth he had gone berserk and bashed the poor fellow, who fled, not even stopping to pick them up.

As a last resort, Reuben's wife paid a secret visit to Dorcas. Dorcas was better at causing toothache than curing it, as it is easier to hurt than to heal, but she told Reuben's wife to put on her husband's boots, stand on level ground under the open sky, catch a frog by its head, spit into its mouth, ask it to take the pain away, then let it go. But this ceremony must be performed on a lucky day at a lucky hour.

'Can you tell me when that is?'

'That will cost you a bit extra, dearie.'

Dorcas went indoors and fetched out a crystal, a beauty on a polished mahogany stand, and duly pronounced that the lucky period would be that very afternoon.

Reuben's wife went back doubtfully through the twisted trees. It was easy to put her husband's boots on, but very difficult to run about in them. Then, was she getting it all in the right order? Did you first stand on level ground, etc., and then stop standing and catch the frog? Or could you catch the frog first? And could you catch it any old how and then hold its head, or must you capture it expressly by its head? It was not easy to spit accurately into a frog's mouth, and Reuben's wife lost command of several mauled and indignant frogs before she came anywhere near completing the ritual. Perhaps by then the lucky hour had run out, because the cure didn't work, and Reuben, in a fresh paroxysm of agony, heaved the front door off its hinges.

Reuben's wife now decided on a desperate course. She would get the young farmer, Simon, the only man anything like strong enough, to seize Reuben from behind and throw him. Three or four other strong men would pile on top of him. As he roared, she would ram her darning mushroom into his mouth to wedge it open, and someone, not yet selected, would go to work with the forceps. It was a wild scheme, and it never got started, because she couldn't get a team together. Simon was reluctant, because he had scruples about attacking an unsuspecting man, but he agreed to play his part because a woman's plea was a command to him. But the other men behaved like horses who won't be brought to the starting post.

Simon gave up and went to the doorway, from where he saw the pale gold head of Sophie Margaret Oakroyd as she went by, and on a sudden impulse he ran out to her.

'Toothache?' she objected. 'I'm not a dentist!'

He replied humbly, 'I believe you have rare powers, Miss.'

'"Rare powers",' repeated Sophie, amused. 'Is that what you think?'

'Will you go to Reuben, Miss?'

She pulled a face. 'If you insist, but I'm not sure I'm up to this.'

A deep hush fell as she approached Reuben's scarred house. She stood for a moment, taking in the glowering bulk of the blacksmith, who sat on a low stool with his hand pressed to his face, and Reuben's wife, tremblingly concealing the forceps behind her back.

'Well,' she said, in a resigned and neutral voice, 'you'd better fetch some warm water and a sponge.' She added, as Reuben's wife stood there, apparently paralysed, 'Warm, not too hot, blood heat.'

9

She poured a little of the water into a cup, and into it she dropped two little white tablets, which fizzed.

'Drink this, please.'

Reuben looked like a beast about to spring, but he lowered his gaze before the blue eyes, took the cup surlily, and drank.

'They're supposed to be instantaneous,' remarked Sophie doubtfully to the gaping onlookers, 'but we'll wait a minute or two. Will you all please be quite quiet?'

And she waited, rather pale but perfectly composed, while Simon stood guard lest Reuben should start bashing her as he had bashed the tooth-drawer. But Reuben, though still sullen and suspicious, seemed curiously subdued.

'*Complete* quiet, please,' said Sophie.

She drew up another stool in front of Reuben, and from around her neck she took a gold chain with a pendant which flashed with the same colour as her eyes. She gave Simon a quick, wry glance.

'Here's hoping,' she said.

She began swinging the pendant slowly to and fro before Reuben's face, like a pendulum.

'Forget the pain,' she murmured, in a voice so low that only Reuben could hear. 'Forget, forget, forget.'

Still swinging the pendant, she continued in this way for some time. Forget, forget, forget, forget . . .

She stopped, and stared long and hard into his face. Then, in a quiet, clear voice, she said:

'You will lie on that couch and hang your head over the side and open your mouth wide. I am going to take your bad tooth out. You will feel nothing, nothing at all, and when I wake you your pain will be gone.'

Reuben rose and plodded like a sleepwalker to the

couch, where he lay with his mouth wide open. The bad tooth was on the left side of the lower jaw, showing a nasty black cavity, and cushioned by inflamed gum.

Sophie took the forceps from the shaking hands of Reuben's wife, and stood for a few moments like a chess player considering a move. An involuntary gasp of horror went up as, on a sudden decision, she pushed the cruel, hooked instrument into Reuben's mouth and worked it over the agonised tooth itself. Simon bunched his muscles, certain that as the cold steel touched him Reuben would leap up mad with pain. He lay there tranquil as a sleeping child. Sophie rammed the pincers past the pitifully swollen gum. She levered to and fro, side to side. Blood welled up and ran out of the side of Reuben's mouth to splash on the floor. She levered and wrenched and tugged. Reuben lay back as if lost in a far off lovely dream.

The big molar was deeply rooted. Sophie wrestled with it with no more restraint than Prudence had shown in wrenching out the crooked nails. The on-lookers winced and grimaced and turned away. Simon's eyes were bolting. And still Reuben lay beatific and bland, and still Sophie laboured on. Then she suddenly jerked back, holding the forceps up with the great four-pronged tooth dripping in their steel beak.

A great sigh went up. Sophie laid aside the tooth, took the basin of warm water and sponge from Reuben's weeping wife, and began gently bathing her patient's mouth and face.

'You can wake up now,' she said, and held her head in her hands for a moment.

Reuben sat up. He experimented with his tongue and touched his face gingerly with his fingers. A look of enormous relief settled on his ham-like features. But then, strangely, instead of pouring out his gratitude, he

looked afraid; he stared at Sophie with a kind of resentment, as if she had humiliated him. Then he lowered
his eyes and mumbled his thanks, and made her the
offer of a newly-shod horse.

'No thank you,' she said politely. Everyone was silent.
Even Reuben's wife was silent.

'She put a magic spell on him,' said someone at last,
hoarsely.

'A sort of spell,' said Sophie patiently, 'but not magic.
Hypnosis.'

'Hip-nose-iss,' they whispered fearfully.

She glanced round, taking in their expressions. Her
abilities were common enough in her own land, but
unknown here, and she had supposed that, if ever she
were called upon to use them, there would be a rush of
eager sufferers begging her for cures. But they were
stunned and silent.

'Well!' she said to Reuben, 'I hope you won't miss
your tooth too much. I think you were secretly in love
with it, you know. Well, good-bye.'

Mysterious words. The people shuddered. They were
chilled with awe, and hostile.

But no, that is not wholly true. There were one or two
young men in the crowd. And they were thrilled by
her.

Simon was standing by humbly.

'I'll see you home, Miss,' he said.

She talked to him as they went, asking him about
himself. He answered civilly but volunteered nothing.
She learned that he was an orphan and had run the
farm, single-handed, from the age of fifteen. She had to
speak to him over her shoulder, because he persistently
walked two paces behind her.

'Walk beside me, Simon, it makes conversation easier.'

But he inclined his head and still hung back.

'Simon, what I did was nothing out of the ordinary.'

'I think it was a miracle, Miss.'

'That's just because it was new to you. Really, there's no miracle about it. Anyone could learn to do it.'

'I think you have a divine gift, Miss.'

His quaint language charmed her. She turned and faced him. They were out in the country now, in warm sunshine, beside a field with a haystack. He was handsome, with his strong body and his lion's mane of tawny hair.

'You're sweet,' she said.

He stood mute and still.

She held out her arms. 'Simon. Come here.'

But he stood where he was, and with a pang of misgiving she saw the change in his face. Nevertheless she persisted. 'Simon, come on.'

He was now looking at her feet. 'That would be unseemly, Miss.'

'"Unseemly"!' It was as archaic as' 'divine'. 'Don't boys kiss girls in this country, then?'

'Not on so brief an acquaintance, Miss.'

'When do they get round to it, then?'

'They are introduced, they keep company for a time, and then they plight their troth.'

'"Plight their troth"!' she repeated, marvelling.

She was still mechanically holding out her arms, but now she let them fall slowly to her sides.

'I've embarrassed you,' she said ruefully.

'That's all right, Miss.'

She gave him a long, wondering stare, then turned away. They went on in silence.

Chapter Two

The hag Dorcas pottered about outside her hovel, making a hell-broth, more or less for the hell of it. Her hovel was such only on the outside, for the sake of appearances, with a rickety chimney, blackened planks held together by poisoned ivy, filthy windows, and a door hung about with dried portions of various small disgusting animals. The inside, which was seen by no-one except herself and her cat, was sumptuously furnished and carpeted wall to wall, and contained cabinets of beautiful silver, bought out of donations from her many clients.

She sang to herself as she stirred the broth:

> *I rather like rats and spiders*
> *And things that do people harm;*
> *The vultures in the zoo*
> *May look horrible to you,*
> *But for me they have a certain charm.*
> *I rather like deadly nightshade*
> *And the nettle's spiteful touch;*
> *They appeal to me*
> *To a certain degree,*
> *But I don't like anything much.*

Dorcas had not always been a hag. In fact it was a

sore point with her, and when the prissy little enchanted princesses minced up with such speeches as, 'Good old mother, I would fain seek counsel from your withered lips', it was all she could do not to turn them into toads; but of course, business was business. Many, many years ago she had been beautiful, with raven hair and fine white teeth, although she had to be careful how she smiled, lest she exposed the eye-teeth, which were unnaturally long and sharp. But time had watched her over the years with a blasé and sardonic eye, seeing her back grow humped and her fingers gnarled, and the tip of her nose meet the point of her chin. She had long ceased to ask the mirror, 'Who is the fairest of them all?' – for what was the use of kidding? – and settled for being a hag, profitably, in the long run. But in spite of all, she hated being old.

She dropped the eye of a newt into the broth and sang another verse:

> *I rather like headless spectres*
> *Lugubrious in the night,*
>   *And the hanged remains*
>   *Of a corpse in chains*
> *Afford me some delight;*
> *I rather like werewolves, vampires,*
> *Clubfooted ghouls and such;*
>   *They please me, I confess,*
>   *But not to excess,*
> *For I don't like anything much.*

She cackled, causing her drowsing cat to open its eyelids sharply over clean, cold eyeballs. She'd fixed that little prig Prudence! Fancy thinking she could catch out an old hand with that worn-out trick! But then she scowled, and the cat deflected its ears slightly, so that it looked like an owl. That girl, that blonde girl, had set Prudence free. She must know a thing or two. And then there was the matter of Reuben's tooth. The spell she had put on him must be stronger than any Dorcas herself could muster. And she was so young, too.

Then Dorcas began to seethe with envy like a Welsh rarebit under a grill. Of all the deadly sins, envy is the least rewarding. Dorcas felt quite ill with it. Young? The creature was not young! She was probably thousands of years old, a super witch with the last secret of all found out.

How to regain lost youth! Ah, to know that!

No good asking her as one witch to another. Witches are ruled by fiends, and there's no trusting fiends; they tell you little truths to let you down in a big way later on.

Dorcas dropped in the fillet of a fenny snake and brooded, while the cat looked on with cold attention. This was a powerful rival and she must proceed cautiously. But she must proceed.

'I must have your blood, my duckie,' she muttered.

Prudence was in bed, convalescing. In that melancholy languor that follows 'flu, she could think of only one subject. Simon, Simon, Simon . . .

He had held her arm. It was the first time in her life that a man had touched her. He had been warm and gentle and strong.

'Don't take advantage of me!' – 'No fear of that, lass!' What did he mean? That he was unmoved by her? Or could it possibly mean that he held her specially dear? She had repeated his words to herself a hundred times.

He had meant nothing. He had taken her arm because he had been asked to. He didn't care. She didn't care,

16

either. She was above such vulgar feelings. She was glad she was going to be a priestess, a dedicated virgin. If he thought he could seduce her he was grossly mistaken.

But hadn't he once asked her, 'Don't you ever want any other kind of job?' Why had he asked that? Had he – had he – even been hinting that she should *marry* him? Her excitement neared to panic. Did God, after all, *not* intend her to become a priestess? Did He actually intend her to be an honourable farmer's wife? Was her mission to provide that fine young man with a righteous and sober mate?

And, yes, to protect him. Protect him from that wicked girl. Prudence had heard the tale of Reuben's tooth. There was witchcraft! Unmistakable! And the Elders ignored it! With a stab of anguish she recalled learning that Simon had gone off with the witch afterwards . . . She would try to seduce him. Horror! – perhaps she already had!

In her run-down state, Prudence became near-delirious. Her mind saw obscene pictures till her heart thundered and she blushed all the way down to her waist. Her mission was imperative. Her appointed husband was in mortal danger and she must save him. Her pathetic solicitude for him turned her heart to jelly. She wept.

Simon finished grooming the great shire horse and then stood lost in thought by its head for so long that the compassionate beast gave him a huge flabby kiss to console him. He shifted absentmindedly and went on thinking.

He could not forget Sophie's crestfallen face as she had stood with her arms outstretched and received no response. At the time she had shocked him. Only the lowest kind of girl (there were a few such in Urstwile) would have acted as she had done. But when he recalled the hurt surprise on her face, he knew she was innocent. To the pure all things were pure.

Innocent, yes. Her miraculous powers must come from that innocence. She was a child of Nature, in touch with the Great Mother's wonderful ways of healing. What kind of land did she come from? It must be a paradise of purity.

And he, he had responded with the sordid suspicion of his race. He felt corrupt, as if he had taken a low advantage of her. How could he apologise? She would not even understand. Yet he must warn her about his world, and protect her too, for such sweet simplicity, at large in this loathsome valley, ran terrible risks.

Sophie went upstairs, took off her Urstwile-fashion dress to reveal underwear that would have outraged the Urstwileans, and put on a dressing-gown. As she had expected, reaction was now setting in from her piece of surgery on Reuben, and her heart raced and she trembled. She lay down, drew a deep, deep breath, and let it out by stages, till on the last exhalation her body collapsed like a pricked balloon. She thought of bright oranges in green trees. She continued in this way until her nerves were calm, but her thoughts still troubled her.

She had behaved very rashly. She had interfered with local life. Twice. If the authorities back home had happened to be monitoring her movements, her father and she could be ordered back at once, no arguing.

Yet what else could she have done? Leave that stupid girl pinned to the ground in the rain? Leave that great oaf of a blacksmith in agony, wreaking havoc?

Her father must never hear of what she had done. Not that it should be difficult to keep it from him.

The world in the Twenty-second Century A.D., of whose girlhood Sophie was a healthy specimen, was no paradise. It was riddled with war, crime, unemployment, strikes and sexual disorder, and bore witness, like all the other centuries before it, to the lunacy of man and the more or less continual chaos of human existence. But in two fields it had reached perfection.

One was the field of thought-therapy or psychological healing. Since teaching of the three R's in the schools had been replaced by Yoga, even an immature, average scholar like Sophie could perform feats of healing which in previous centuries would have been thought miracles.

The second was the field of Conservation. The feverishly muddled Twentieth Century had sent its crude television gangs into every corner of the globe to poke their noses into the lives of primitive peoples, and the reaction to this interference had contributed to the great social upheaval of the appalling Twenty-first Century. But the Twenty-second Century had Conservation buttoned up: Conservation *meant* Conservation. So, dotted about the world, there were tiny, backward communities living on in comfortable ignorance, with no more idea of the great world outside than has the worm in one's bloodstream, who is blissfully unaware that the red tide he swims in is not the whole of Creation.

Urstwile was such a community. Its inhabitants thought of 'the world beyond the mountains' only in terms of the haziest dreams and the wildest superstitions.

The Twenty-second Century watched its Conservation pockets mainly from afar, but occasionally – very rarely – a great scholar would be allowed to visit a community in person. Professor Oakroyd was such a scholar. He was writing a book that would be the official study of the Urstwileans, and he needed personal contact with his subject. Not that he contacted much, now that he was here. He stayed indoors, did exercises to keep fit, viewed the life of Urstwile on master screens, and wrote notes in longhand, writing having returned to favour as a means of expression. Sophie supplied his personal contacts.

She had been allowed to accompany him because she was essential to his existence, as he found ordinary life bewildering and unnerving. She was there to cook for him, see that he changed his socks, and prevent him from falling over chairs when lost in thought.

You could buy lovely old things like real hens' eggs in the markets of Urstwile, and Sophie cooked a delicious concoction that evening. She herself, however, was off her food. She was still worried. There was something else.

Before coming here she had been carefully primed in Urstwilean customs, but you can't think of everything, and some points had been overlooked. She could not forget Simon's face when she had held out her arms to him and then embarrassingly had had to return them empty to her sides. She should have found his reaction comic, but she could not. She had had a glimpse of unguessed-at qualities: delicacy of feeling, self-respect, respect for herself and her sex. It moved her, and, although it was quite unfair to herself, she felt she had behaved cheaply; and for some unfathomable reason, she found herself longing for his approval.

Well, the correct procedure was to write about it, to write it out of herself, as the saying had it. She got out her alphabetically tabulated exercise book, opened it at the letter C, and wrote the archaic word 'Chivalry' for a heading – putting it in inverted commas, of course. But she was stuck for words, and gave up. She laid her head on her arms. A lump rose in her throat. She had never felt like this in her life before, and not even thinking of bright oranges in green trees could cure her of it.

Chapter Three

'The Oakroyd girl –' began the Chief Elder.

'Yessir. The ash-blonde witch, sir,' said the spy.

'That is prejudicial language,' said the Chief Elder sternly, 'and most improper.'

'Yessir.'

'You will refer to her as Miss Oakroyd.'

'Yessir. Sorry, sir.'

'Have you investigated the cottage?'

'Yessir. I went disguised as a dustman, sir. Funny thing is, sir, they don't have any dustbins. They've got some contraption, sir, that sort of spirits the garbage away. The place is full of peculiar junk, sir.'

'You mean the paraphernalia of witchcraft?'

'Well, not like Dorcas's stuff, no, sir.'

'I have no idea of what "Dorcas's stuff" may be like,' snapped the Chief Elder.

'No, of course not, sir. Sorry, sir.'

'Have you reached any conclusion as to how they got here?'

'Not really, sir. They *do* say, sir, that they escaped from a riven oak, sir. Riven by lightning, sir. Night of the storm. They *do* say the man and his daughter were imprisoned in that tree for hundreds of years, sir, and –'

'That is idle gossip,' said the Chief Elder.

'Yessir.'

'You will avoid idle gossip.'

'Yessir. Sorry, sir.'

'However, you will reconnoitre that region, and take careful note of riven oaks. You may go.'

The Chief Elder pondered. He was a just man. Under his guidance Urstwile was politer and more orderly than it had ever been in its history. He hoped to keep it so. He hated rumours. Yet, in all conscience, they were excusable in this case. The Oakroyds' cottage: how, from being a run-down little shack, empty for years, had it suddenly become spick and span, with fresh paint and a new thatch? It was as if – he flinched from even thinking it – it was as if someone had waved a magic wand over it.

The girl had performed some strange acts.

They had been acts of mercy, to be sure.

Yet the powers of darkness sometimes did a little good in order to do great harm.

Not having had visitors in living memory, he was not sure how to treat these two. He must certainly keep an eye on them.

It was the custom for the poets of Urstwile to fix their poems to the notice board in the central square of the capital town, doing so as a rule in the quiet of night, and omitting to sign them. They would hang about on the edges of crowds to get the people's reaction. If this was favourable they would modestly own up to the authorship, and if bad, slink away.

Urstwile poetry was almost always in ballad form, describing personal heroism in conventional language:

> *He rushed at me, athirst for blood,*
> *But I sprang aside with a cat-like leap;*

I thumped his head with a sickening thud,
And he fell in a crumpled heap.

But one morning a new kind of poem appeared, in a strange and sensuous metre:

> *One warm night*
> *I was walking round the garden*
> *When an ash-blonde witch*
> *Pinned me to a tree;*
> *Knife in hand*
> *Amid the great red roses,*
> *She was looking for a lover*
> *And she picked on me.*
>
> *Murderous, murderous*
> *The great red roses,*
> *With long dark thorns*
>
> *To tear me apart;*
> *O angel with a rapier*
> *– Jill the Ripper –*
> *You were looking for a lover,*
> *And you broke my heart.*
>
> *One warm night*
> *I was walking round a bedroom,*
> *Looking for a bosom*
> *To pillow my head,*
> *When an ash-blonde witch*
> *Who was looking for a lover*
> *With her mind on murder*
> *Cut me dead.*

The critics who were gathered round the board were scandalised. It was obscure. It was morbid. It was decadent. It was obscene. One critic declared loudly that he would rather give his daughter a dose of poison than permit her to gaze upon such filth.

But a group of young men, craning to read it past the critics' shoulders, were overtaken by madness. Before any official had time to rip the evil poem from the board, they linked arms four abreast and marched down the high street, frightening the horses, impeding the traffic, and chanting in a kind of delirium:

> *Murderous, murderous,*
> *The great red roses . . .*

Women shook their fists and shouted curses and stuffed their fingers in their daughters' ears. A few arrests were made, some fines were imposed, and the young men were quickly restored to modesty. But the damage was done. No fingers had been stuffed in the young girls' ears hard enough to prevent them from learning the wicked words themselves, and pretty soon they were crooning '*murderous, murderous*' under their breath as they did the housework, and it came near to causing real murder in their homes, where there were scenes of thundering rage, storms of tears, diabolical threats, and harsh decrees. Urstwile had never come so near to a generation war.

The Elders huddled together in conclave. It was obvious who the witch in the poem was meant to be, even though the poet called her Jill. But what had she done wrong? Nothing. The young people were fascinated by her, and if she were hastily condemned she would become a martyr in their eyes.

The Elders were long in the tooth. They knew that the best way of provoking people to act is to forbid them to do so. They therefore let it be known that any hostility to Miss Sophie Oakroyd, whether in the form of insults, injury, or even insinuation, would be immediately and severely punished. Having thus fastened down the lid, they waited for the cauldron to boil. If mob action were taken, and the girl was lynched, they would always claim that they had tried to prevent it.

Meanwhile they hunted for the author of the poem. All the known poets went through a trying time. Their houses were searched; they were interrogated in the small hours of the morning. But fortunately for them, their literary styles were well enough known for it to be agreed that none of them could possibly have been responsible.

Dorcas, away in her hovel, chuckled to herself. She had just obtained the scale of a dragon (very hard to come by), to add to the hell-broth, so she was pleased. But still more pleased was she with her latest literary effort. As has already been seen, she was a neat hand at turning verses. Her latest one was having quite a run.

Sophie seemed extraordinarily obtuse. Young people, especially young men, gazed on her with eyes brimming with suppressed excitement, and older people, especially women, gazed on her with eyes brimming with suppressed hatred, yet she noticed nothing. She went about in a distracted way, speaking in a faraway voice, bumping into people, and generally behaving as if lost in a dream. As indeed she was. But she couldn't bring herself to speak to Simon, other than giving him a distant 'good morning', for fear of offending him again.

Her dreamy air aroused everybody. The young thought it glamorous, and girls began imitating it. Their elders thought it shameless. No-one, least of all Simon himself, knew the cause of it. To him, it was just

another sign of her injured innocence. She was bewildered and hurt, poor little thing, by the strange
looks that were thrown at her. How could she read the
crooked hearts of the Urstwileans? But he did not speak
to her, for fear that his own clumsiness might make
matters worse.

Prudence, now well enough to go out, noted the
distant, brief exchanges between the two of them, and
was much heartened.

Until, that is, she looked in her mirror. Her appearance was sober and righteous all right, but not alluring.
She was far from ugly – a bit thin, but well-featured,
with fine eyes – but she was not making the best of her
looks. Expression – worthy, certainly, but – how to
describe it, in a word? – frankly, boring. Dress, boring.
Hair, boring.

She was convinced that she had divine support in
her pursuit of Simon, and this was a great advantage, of
course, but perhaps a future husband had to be attracted
by other qualities than sobriety and righteousness?
Well, was not the body the Temple of the Spirit?
Couldn't temples be done up a bit?

Dorcas had a pang of misgiving. She suspected that the
scale of a dragon, for which she had paid through the
nose, might be from an iguana or even a young alligator.
There was frightful cheating in the trade. She told
herself that things were going well, that she shouldn't
grumble, but her spirit continued to grumble nevertheless. She sat in her parlour and polished a silver
bowl till it shone like white light. It was no good. Her
misgiving became more than a pang, nor was the
dragon's scale the cause of it. Her thumbs began pricking and throbbing. Her mouth went dry. Her hair stood
on end. She felt ill. She stumbled to the hovel door,

panting for air, and leaned against the lintel. The mummified leg of a lizard swung and brushed her face.

Her black cat started up out of sleep, saw something, and stared. Its fur crackled and its eyes went black with terror. It rushed out of doors as if devils had called. As indeed they had.

Chapter Four

'A charming people, aren't they?' said Professor Oakroyd.

'Some of them,' said Sophie.

'Oh, in general, I'd say.'

'But you never meet any of them.'

'No, I think that would be a mistake; one might be tempted to draw general conclusions from particular cases. I prefer to observe them in the mass. Their cultural customs are fascinating. Did you know that the poets recite their poems in the market square, like the Ancient Greeks? And that the people will march through the streets arm in arm declaiming them? Charming, isn't it? Their very backwardness keeps them happy, of course. My belief has always been that civilisation corrupts. Look at us, with our advanced technology! Are we happy?'

'No, we aren't,' said Sophie, with feeling.

'Oh, but,' said the professor, put out by being brought down to a particular case, *'you're* all right, aren't you? I mean, not homesick or anything, are you?'

'Homesick? Oh, no.'

'That's good.' He had noticed, vaguely, that she had been mopey of late. Off her food. 'Well, in any case, we'll only be here for another week or two.'

'Oh, great,' said Sophie forlornly.

'Cheer up. Think positively. There are things one can learn from these people.'

'Yes, there are,' she agreed.

'That's the way to look at it. Their remarkable gentleness, for instance. Their utter lack of malice.'

A day had passed since the cat had behaved so strangely. The moon was rising behind the rheumaticky trees of Cankered Wood, blighting their black deformities with the sheen of leprosy. It was an ominous, haunted scene, but it did nothing for Dorcas, who was unimpressed by the creator's work either at dawn or sunset; she thought it rather flashy.

The black cat rose and stretched and prepared for its nightly prowl. But when Dorcas opened the door the animal would go no farther, but remained stuck in an awkward attitude, the moonlight making hellish discs of its eyes. Dorcas looked at it with misgiving. Something was disturbing it. She was disturbed herself; not for nothing did her thumbs start pricking. Something nasty was in the offing. The trouble with being a witch was that you kept thinking of the devil, and when you thought of him, he appeared, or his minions did, and they were just as likely to do mischief *to* you as *for* you.

This time, however, something human had caught the cat's attention: the sound of approaching footsteps. In due course the moonlight disclosed the Chief Elder, imperfectly disguised as a woodcutter, in a brand new leather jerkin and green hose. The effect was spoiled by his Elder's sash of office, which he could never bring himself to leave off, even in bed.

He looked downwards out of the sides of his eyes, and began in a sepulchral voice:

'How now, you secret, black and mid –'

'Yes, all right,' said Dorcas testily. She detested the words he was going to say. 'What brings you here? Your floosie making too many demands again, is she?'

'I don't know what you mean,' he replied haughtily. 'I come to seek your counsel.'

'You'll pay up for it, then, coming at this hour. Who do you want done down this time?'

'I want no-one "done down",' he said with dignity, drawing himself up, although not very high, for he was short and fat, 'and your question was uncalled for. You have heard of our visitor, Sophie Margaret Oakroyd?'

'Might have.' Dorcas looked at him askance. The cat, who had shown him sleepy contempt so far, opened its eyes wide in a cold attentive stare.

'She has rare powers,' said the Chief Elder soberly.

'She's done a couple of parlour tricks,' said Dorcas begrudgingly.

'You must know what effect she is having on the people.'

'Must I?'

'We want to know what she is, and where she comes from.'

'Better ask her.'

'I'll be frank. Is she one of your sisterhood?'

'What sisterhood?'

'Oh, come —'

'I didn't know I had any sisters,' said Dorcas. 'I thought I was a poor old woman living all on her own.'

This conversation was full of evasions and denials, which was only to be expected, as Dorcas was hardly likely to admit to being a witch, nor the Chief Elder to seeking the help of one, but some sort of agreement had to be reached, or it would get nowhere. The Chief Elder produced a small leather bag and shook out a few coins that winked yellow in the moonlight. In the same movement, as if she were his partner in a dance, Dorcas

31

slipped out a skinny hand, and the coins disappeared.

'How should I know what she is?'

'You have the wisdom and experience of your great age.'

He intended a compliment, but Dorcas snarled at him.

'So?'

'Oh, come on,' said the Chief Elder, tired of this, 'is she a witch or isn't she?'

Dorcas looked aside to hide her satisfaction. Did the old fool really expect an honest opinion?

'Shall I speak, or shall we ask the advice of others?'

'Call them up,' said the Chief Elder darkly.

Dorcas chuckled softly. How well things were going! A little powder sprinkled on her fire to turn the flames green, a bit of ventriloquism, and she could gain two ends: the elimination of her rival, and, with a bit of luck, a pint or two of her blood, drinking which (plus a few preservatives) could give Dorcas back her youth. She was so pleased that she hummed a few lines of her song, 'I rather like rats and spiders', as she fetched the powder.

'Now,' she said, 'don't speak to what you see. The powers know your thoughts.' And having thus prevented any difficult questions, she sprinkled some powder round the base of the cauldron, from which evil-smelling steam was rising.

But at this point, quite beyond her intention, the powers of darkness really did intervene – although 'powers' might give a wrong impression. As has already been seen, there were demons in the vicinity of the hovel, and they had caused Dorcas's thumbs to prick and the cat to panic. But powerful they were not. They were a shambling, furtive lot, and the despair of their masters, who had given them a beat in Cankered Wood just to keep them into mischief. They were depressingly stupid and quite irresponsible, fit only for smashing things up. They were also very bored, which causes devilment. When they saw the green flames begin to flicker around Dorcas's cauldron they rushed upon them with oafish howls of delight. They turned her modest little conflagration into a great column of green, yellow and vermilion smoke in which fantastic figures writhed, indefinable, because they kept drunkenly changing shape: dragons, black horses snorting fire, a great twisted cat with splayed and dripping claws. They bombarded one another with foul jests, although it was impossible to make out what they were saying, as the diction of minor demons is deplorable. Each low sally was greeted with a gust of coarse laughter. It was a disgusting exhibition. But Dorcas and her cat were aghast.

'Elementals!' croaked Dorcas. 'They are elementals!'

'Elementals?' repeated the Chief Elder, much perturbed. 'Do you mean by that, primitive earth-spirits which –'

'What do you think I am, you old fool, a dictionary? *Run!*'

And she dashed into her hovel with the cat, and turned keys, and shot bolts, and fixed chains. An attentive listener would have heard her babbling incantations from within. But the Chief Elder heard only the howling of fiends, and saw only the circus of monsters, and ran, and ran, and ran.

At this time the trees of Cankered Wood decided to join in the fun. When the Chief Elder was approaching the hovel, they had been on their best behaviour, in rigid attitudes, as if rooted to the spot. But now they began to imitate the actions of chessmen, and castled, and made the knight's move, so that the wood was like a kaleidoscope in motion. To the Chief Elder, it was as if he were running madly in all directions at once. He developed a stitch. When he tried to recover his breath by leaning against a tree, it side-stepped and he fell on his back. How he progressed from there on is not known. He was never seen in Urstwile again. Presumed lost.

The people in the town crept trembling to their windows to look at the frightful symbols in the sky. Professor Oakroyd went to his window too. He called Sophie, but she was asleep. He noted the phenomenon with great satisfaction. 'They have invented fireworks,' he said to himself.

After a short while the minor demons, typically, became bored again, and the manifestations ceased. The next day, all seemed normal; but some strange things began to happen in Urstwile. Gabriel, one of the best poets in the kingdom, was trying to write a poem. He was famous for his stirring, warlike ballads. This one began promisingly:

> *Ho, trumpets, sound a war-note!*
> *Ho, lictors, clear the way!*

But by the third line, the thing began to get a bit rocky:

> *Ho, bang the drum! Ho, let-em-all-come!*

And in the fourth, it collapsed completely:

> *Ho! . . . well, ho, anyway . . .*

Gabriel put down his pen and burst into tears.

A cross-legged tailor, making a coat, found that he had sewn all the buttonholes up. A milkman ignored the out-held jug of his customer and poured a gallon of milk carefully over her feet. A mouse, pounced on by a cat, turned on it and chased it up a tree.

Prudence had been experimenting daily before her mirror. She was trying to get exactly the right quantities and shades of make-up, so that she would look like a rose in June without anyone's seeing that she had it on at all. This morning, after concentrating hard, she found that she had plastered her lips and her cheeks with vermilion, her eyelids with blue, and her lashes with black, so that each one stuck out like a little peg. The mask of a Scarlet Woman leered at her from her glass! She turned deadly pale beneath this coating. She thought she saw the blue, blue eyes of Sophie Oakroyd, mocking her, behind her own reflection. She felt the witch's hand guiding her own. She wept, and her face looked as if it had been left out in the rain. 'Oh Simon, Simon, my intended,' she sobbed, 'how shall we rid ourselves of her evil toils?'

Simon was leading the great horse out of its stable when it bit him on the upper arm. He turned and looked at it in astonishment. It stared back at him in embarrassment and shame.

'Something's wrong,' he murmured, and stood distractedly stroking the abject creature.

When, he decided, a girl like Sophie, like a visiting angel, brought her pure flame of beauty to a place like Urstwile, and did wonderful deeds of good, it unsettled them, it was more than they could stand. For days now the town had been twitching and rustling with unrest, and clearly things were getting worse.

He did not know that in Sophie's country hundreds

35

of girls just like her poured out of the colleges every day, bouncy, beautiful, in perfect health, and almost exactly alike. To him she was unique.

He sensed the gathering storm. He sensed her danger. Badly though he had treated her, he must make her listen to him, he must warn her.

Chapter Five

The Elders of Urstwile believed, as a general rule, in letting sleeping dogs lie; but the disappearance of the Chief could hardly be ignored. Therefore, even before he had stopped rushing about Cankered Wood, colliding with trees, they put it about that he had perished while carrying out a breathtakingly daring investigation of witchcraft which had led him into regions where the foot of man had never trod. They were skilled in putting things about. Soon the citizens were telling one another that the Chief Elder had been seen, in woodland garb, swirling about at the head of a three hundred foot column of green smoke in an aerial menagerie which included a dragon, several savage horses, and a cat.

They decided not to follow him into Cankered Wood themselves. If they all disappeared too, leaving Urstwile with no-one at the helm, how would the country manage to drift along?

Rumour is seldom reasonable. It began now to link Sophie with Dorcas. The two women, it whispered, were in league. Dorcas was known to give people toothache when the mood took her. Sophie had *cured* toothache. A suspicious connection there, wasn't there? The Elders, at a loss without their Chief, began importunately to interrogate people. Reuben, the blacksmith, was one. You might think that Reuben would be eternally grateful to Sophie? This was not the case. Reuben was, be it admitted, solid bone between his ears. He had a fixed idea about the role of women in society; it was that they had no role in society. Being cured by a woman, not to mention a slip of a girl, humiliated him. His friends, whom he occasionally entertained by twisting horseshoes in half (the friends of strong men are notoriously easy to entertain) pulled his leg unceasingly about it. When the Elders questioned him, he was surly.

'What did she say before she began operating on you?'

'"Here's hoping".'

'And afterwards?'

'"Hip-nose-iss".'

'Did these strike you as mystic words?'

'Yer.'

'How did you feel when she swung the pendant before your eyes?'

'Funny.'

'Did you feel that she was bewitching you?'

'Yer.'

'Why did you not stop her? Were you at her mercy?'

'Yer.'

'So she could have commanded you to do anything, and you would have had to obey?'

'Reckon so, yer.'

'Does such power seem evil to you?'

'Yer.'

Reuben's wife interrupted, timidly, 'Well, I'm very grateful to the young lady, I am. I've had peace ever since she took his tooth out, I have. He was in such pain, heart-rendering, it was. Carried on something awful, he did. You've no idea, you haven't –'

The interrogating Elder turned coldly on her.

38

'You visited the witch Dorcas.'

'Well, but lots of people do, now and again, they do –'

'Indeed? Name them.'

'Oh no, I couldn't do that, not as you might say name them, I couldn't –'

'Were you to name them, they would be stood in the pillory.'

'Oh dear, I'm sure I wouldn't want that to happen, I wouldn't.'

'I shall overlook what you have told me, but be careful in future.'

'Oh yes, sir, I'll be careful, I will.'

As has been seen, Sophie had in a very short while become the centre of a cult for the young people of Urstwile. Did they now close their ranks in her support? They did not. They were dependent on their elders for their upkeep, and they soon decided what was prudent for them to do. What had been an exciting novelty had become a dangerous risk. They put aside their follies. The moral is, never assume that The People are on your side. It has been the downfall of many a man.

Simon was questioned too. His steady answers silenced the Elders for the time being, but, of course, the matter was soon to pass far beyond the stage of tactical question and answer. Simon knew this. His mind made up, he waylaid Sophie when next she left the cottage, and stopped her in her tracks.

'I must talk to you, Miss Oakroyd.'

'All right, Simon.' She was thrilled, but she kept a cool manner. 'What shall we talk about?'

'We must not talk in the open. You see that barn just across the field. Meet me there. Keep close to the hedge as you go.'

'Right,' said Sophie, with pleasant anticipation.

But when they met in the barn it was not as she had expected. He leaned against the wheel of a farm cart, gazed steadily into her face, and talked in low, earnest tones.

'A witch?' she repeated. She was rather pleased. 'Is that what they think? Aren't they sweet?'

'*Sweet*!' he echoed grimly. 'The mood they're in isn't at all sweet, I assure you.'

'Simon, I never saw such a well-behaved town. Compared to it, my home town's a jungle.'

'Your jungle has some lovely creatures in it.'

'You talk like a story-book,' she said, delightedly. 'I think Urstwile is rather like fairyland. Wicked witches. Magic spells. It's too good to be true.'

'You must take me seriously.'

'Come to think of it, some pretty horrible things are done to witches in fairy tales.' She remembered one where the witch was bounced down a hill in a barrel full of nails. 'Good heavens, what do you think they'd do to me? Burn me?'

'It's quite possible,' he replied gravely.

'Simon! Those people? Those nice, gentle people?' She turned pale. 'Have you ever seen anyone burned?'

'No, it hasn't happened for many years, but it could happen now. They are in the mood for it.'

'Then they'd better get out of the mood, quickly. There are no such things as witches.'

'Not in your "jungle", perhaps,' he said, smiling sadly. She had given him a false impression with that word. He visualised her country as a woodland paradise, with an occasional wolf as a hazard. 'But there are here. Dorcas is one.'

'That poor old thing in the pointed hat? All she needs is a good bath and a course of remedial exercises.'

'You say strange things,' he said, shaking his head.

'You *believe* strange things,' she retorted. 'You're like that silly girl who thought she was stuck to the ground. She could have got up any time she wanted. All she needed was for me to tell her so.'

'That was wonderful,' he said soberly. 'Have you the power to "get them out of the mood", as you say? Could you really do that?'

Crowd control. Mass hypnotism. Sophie was not an advanced student and she was not equal to that.

'My people,' she said grimly, 'could wipe them all out.'

Yes, at the touch of a button. All Urstwile. But as she said it she knew they never would, nor intervene in the slightest degree, except perhaps to call her father back in disgrace. Before he left, Professor Oakroyd had had to sign form after form agreeing that he was going *entirely at his own risk*, like a spy into enemy territory. Her world took conservation seriously.

'Tell me about your world,' he said, softly and winningly, as if to a child. He pictured a race living by the laws of some ancient mythology, primitive, possessed of long-forgotten mysteries. He pictured them using bows and arrows. (Urstwile had discovered gunpowder several decades ago.)

Sophie said quickly, 'Simon, I can't do that.'

'Ah!' he replied. Her innocence charmed him at every turn. 'You are forbidden to divulge your mysteries! Your priests forbid it, perhaps?'

'Something like that,' she answered, looking at him in adoration and wonder.

'Anyway,' he said, after a long pause, during which he gazed back with much the same expression as her own, 'you may come from a land where they are too innocent to believe in witches, but you've come to one where they do. Urstwile is cynical and corrupt. They mistake purity for evil.'

41

Sophie laughed, shaking her head incredulously. 'You're lovely,' she said.

'You wished me to kiss you once,' he said gravely.

'Oh, more than once.'

He took her in his arms, as if handling something precious and fragile. Sophie, up-gathered, thought of hens' eggs. You could get real ones in Urstwile. At home they were synthetic. And so were the young men: fine physical specimens, the product of scientific diet and breathing, but gymnasium-made, as it were. Simon was a real human male. This was something new.

Prudence had now got the knack of applying make-up so that it could not be detected, and people began asking her if she'd been on holiday, but still she was not happy. She had somehow lost her nerve, and it made her vulnerable. She had never been popular, least of all with canoodling couples, but she had been proud of her unpopularity. It made her feel superior. People took her at her own value. She was special, she was going to be a priestess. They felt reluctantly humble in her presence. Now that she had lost her confidence they began to take advantage of it, like sparrows pecking a wounded comrade. Unfair though it was, they hinted that she, too, was part of the witchcraft conspiracy. Hadn't she tampered with Dorcas and been freed by the witch Sophie Oakroyd? All in it together, if you ask me. Birds of a feather.

Prudence was not so thick-skinned that she didn't feel the new atmosphere, but what worried her more were her fears about Sophie and Simon. Neither had been into town for some days. The Oakroyds' cottage and Simon's farm were near neighbours. What *was* going on between them? What chance had she against Sophie's evil beauty? She had virtue on her side, of course. Was that much use?

She could stand it no longer; she must seek Simon out and open his eyes to his danger. She put on her new gown, which hung elegantly about her slender figure, as though she were a mannequin, and set off rather self-consciously towards the south and the open country.

'Proper got-up this morning,' said someone in a group of women as she passed. She averted her eyes and hurried on.

'Not speaking to us this morning?' called another.

Prudence had lost the power of making them feel small. She looked back, said 'good morning' with dignity enough to freeze them, but they laughed jeeringly.

'Going for a walk, are we?'

'As far as a certain cottage?'

'A coven there, is there?'

A small stone tapped her heel, and she was not sure whether one of them had tossed it after her, but she did not look back. She was making for the open fields, where she hoped to find Simon working. She climbed a stile and walked along a narrow strip beside the crops, went through a gate, and passed a haystack. Formerly, she had always regarded haystacks as a great provocation to immorality, but now she did just hope, wistfully, that she might meet Simon in the neighbourhood of this one. It would be a good spot to persuade him in.

But he was not near the haystack, so she went on to the nearest barn and looked in. There, before her eyes, the ash-blonde witch held Simon in her arms. And there was no doubting the fact that he, to an equal extent, held her. They were locked together, motionless, like statues, in an endless kiss.

43

'Simon!!'

They broke apart, dazedly, and blinked at her.

She felt a rush of blood to the head. 'Simon, don't! Oh, don't, my beloved! She'll – she'll pin you to a tree!'

Then, like a maiden in a romantic ballad, she fell at their feet in a swoon.

Dorcas, after a prolonged period, crawled out from under the table and tremblingly unfastened her front door. She peered out. The trees were still. Awful, the way they had jumped around of their own accord. The elementals had directed them. Terrifying. This was even worse than when a mentally deficient poltergeist had once got into her cottage, and thrown her silver about.

But who had called up the elementals? Dorcas peered into the hell-broth, still simmering over a volcano of hot ashes, and began to come to terms with herself. She was a highly intelligent woman of sound common sense, and she knew her own limitations. That witch, that ash-blonde witch, was not to be trifled with. She had sensed that Dorcas was going to spin off some lies about her to the Chief Elder, and she had hit back promptly and with force. Few people could call up elementals at will. She was a very powerful witch indeed.

She was certainly not going to be trapped by any scheme that Dorcas could devise. Well, the rule was, if you can't beat 'em, join 'em. Swallowing her pride, Dorcas put on her pointed hat, fetched her broomstick from the shed, straddled it, and soared up vertically to the clouds. Below her, the trees of Cankered Wood stood still, in dejected attitudes. An obliging crow led her to the Oakroyds' cottage by the shortest route.

Chapter Six

'You must have led her on,' said Sophie.

'I did nothing of the sort.'

They faced each other, in rage and misery, over the prostrate form of Prudence.

'Don't be ridiculous,' said Sophie. 'Do you mean to tell me that she'd come all this way, walk right into your barn, call you her beloved, and pass out, without some cause?'

'How am I to know?'

'Of course you know.'

'I tell you –'

'Well, do something, don't just leave her lying here.'

Sophie was experiencing another new emotion: jealousy. The Twenty-second Century had almost eliminated it, along with road accidents and the common cold. Boys and girls intermingled so freely that they had lost the capacity for jealousy, just as they had for lasting affection. In her country one boy was like another.

But Simon was unique. And no-one else could have him. The sight of Prudence, lying in the dust with specks of chaff sticking to her, moved Sophie only with the wish to kick her. And the sight of Simon, bending over her with that tenderness that came so naturally to him, was more than she could stand.

'No doubt you'll have some explaining to do. I'll leave you to it.'

'Don't go! Wait!'

'No, thank you. I've got her out of one mess already. Now you get her out of this one.'

She strode to the doorway.

'I love you,' he called, desperately.

She put her head round the barn door for a parting shot. 'I must say, you've got a right lunatic there,' she said. 'Do you drive all your girls the same way?'

'I love you,' he repeated dully.

Prudence came to just in time to hear this. She sat up and looked at Simon with infinite forgiveness.

'I know you do,' she whispered. 'Thank heaven I came in time.'

Sophie had gone only twenty paces when she realised how rash she had been, leaving Prudence to regain consciousness, no doubt with a show of much pretty reluctance, in Simon's arms. His indignant surprise must have been quite genuine. The girl, a rabid neurotic, was obviously making a dead set at him. Look at that sleazy dress, that frightful stark make-up. And that charade of being stuck to the pavement: plainly a ruse to lure Simon into touching her. (Sophie forgot, in her distress, that Prudence couldn't possibly have held the hammer down against his strength.) She sat down on a boulder by the wayside, breathing hard. In her world, all emotions were described as 'tension'. There were simple home cures for tension. But the thought of bright oranges in green trees merely depressed her.

She thought of something else. Here in Urstwile they believed in witchcraft. Her world called that superstition. But it also taught, psychology being its religion, that it was what you thought that mattered. So: there were real witches in Urstwile, because everyone thought

46

there were. Simon certainly believed in them. Prudence, the future priestess, was just the one to inflate his belief and blacken Sophie's name. And she, Sophie, had left the field clear to her.

She sat for a long time, staring at the ground. She felt hopelessly alien. What chance had her enlightenment in this benighted place?

Oh well: her father and she were to go home in a few days.

Tears began trickling down her cheeks. That would be awful.

She awoke to her true condition, like one who learns that she has a shocking disease. 'I'm in love,' she said bleakly.

She raised her head. A large, melancholy crow flew by. She watched it listlessly. Then she sprang to her feet. From behind a fleecy white cloud, sailed a woman on a broomstick. She wore a pointed hat and her features were hooked and sharp. She planed to the left, so that Sophie saw the yellow symbols on her fluttering skirts; then she disappeared over a ridge of trees, in the direction of the Oakroyds' cottage.

'Hallucination,' faltered Sophie.

But she *had* seen it, plain as – well, plain as the beaky nose on the woman's face.

No. She had been *thinking* about witches, that was all, thinking so hard that her eyes had been made the dupes of other senses.

No. She *had* seen it.

'I'm in love,' she exclaimed suddenly, 'and this illusion is a side-effect.'

Yes, that must be it. Oh, good.

She tramped home, kicking the folds of her full skirt before her.

'Home, Dad,' she called.

No answer.

'Dad?'

She ranged through the house. Her father had gone, and every particle of equipment they had brought for this visit seemed to have gone with him.

The astute reader will have grasped what had happened. Even the dim one will have a vague idea. The authorities at home, of course, had become aware of the disturbance to the peace of Urstwile, not by direct observation (which leads to biased conclusions) but by studying squiggly lines on electronic graphs. The Urstwile squiggly line kept giving little jumps, as if it had hiccoughs. Professor Oakroyd was upsetting the balance in Urstwile, and must be recalled at once.

They never sent live human beings to transport the offenders in these cases. Human beings were corruptible. They sent robots. So it was that, while Sophie and Simon were occupied in the barn, a robot called at the Oakroyds' cottage, having been precipitated there in de-atomised form through the ether at the speed of light, to reassemble itself on the doorstep.

'Return home?' said Professor Oakroyd impatiently. 'My researches are not yet complete.'

'Orders are to return home at once, sir,' said the robot in a cultured voice. Twenty-second Century robots did not speak in thin, metallic monotones, like earlier models.

'I need at least another five days.'

'Orders are to return home at once, sir.'

'I must have time to get my things together.' The professor was already giving in; there was no resisting a robot. You could punch it, kick it or saw it in half; it would make no difference. At best he could play for time.

'Orders are to return home at once, sir.'

'My daughter!' He had known something was missing. 'My daughter's out! We must wait for her!'

'Orders are –' began the robot again, then stopped. There was a whirring of little wheels as his built-in conscience began working. Soon, not perhaps at the speed of light, but more quickly than the speed of human thought, he settled the matter. 'Your daughter,' he said courteously, 'will be recovered in due course.'

'But you can't just leave her here!'

'Your daughter will be recovered in due course.'

'Wait just five minutes!'

'Orders are to return home at once, sir.'

Professor Oakroyd shrugged hopelessly. In a series of swift flashes, so that at times there seemed to be a dozen of him, each slightly overlapping the other, the robot collected together all his belongings and packed them carefully into the sphere that had reformed its particles in the lane outside. He took the professor by the arm and led him gently to the vehicle.

'What pleasant weather we are enjoying,' he remarked affably, as they set off.

'Enjoying it immensely,' said the professor glumly.

'In the summer,' volunteered the robot, 'the sun shines, whereas in the winter we must endure the snow, the ice, and the frost. I prefer the heat to the cold.'

'But my *daughter*,' protested Professor Oakroyd, back home.

'Yes, I know, professor,' said the High Commissioner pacifically, 'it is inconvenient. Fortunately Urstwile is the safest of conservations. We shall bring her home as soon as we can. Although, mind you, it may take a little while. It won't do to send another agent too soon. There's the danger of imbalance. We can't risk that, with the elections so near.'

'Ah yes, the elections,' said Professor Oakroyd gloomily.

'It would be playing into the hands of the Neo-Radicals.'

'Yes.' Professor Oakroyd had no interest in politics. He knew that the Neo-Radicals were a weirdly discontented lot, for everything that was against and against everything that was for.

'But, High Commissioner, the *girl*.'

'Look,' said the High Commissioner, 'we can fit you up with a supply daughter for the time being. Would that appeal to you?'

'No, it would not,' snapped the professor, and left the room.

'Unfortunate, that,' said the High Commissioner to his robot secretary. 'I've had my doubts about him for some time. Too prone to get emotionally involved.'

'The heart has its reasons,' said the robot secretary, 'which reason does not know about.'

'Yes, I know,' said the High Commissioner, frowning. 'We shall have to change all that.'

Sophie realised at once what had happened to her father, but she was not consoled. Here she was, with her hair grown long for the visit, and clad in a fancy-dress gown with a breast-plate of smocking on the bodice, but conspicuously foreign nevertheless, and evidently unpopular: the inhabitants wanted to burn her. Deprived of the aids of her own civilisation, she was as helpless as a baby. And she had just stormed out on her only friend.

Was she deprived? Well, she could get in touch with her father on the bead-sized walkie-talkie she wore round her neck in the form of a pendant, but it would be most unwise to do so while he was still with the robot. If the suggestion leaked out that she was frightened and wanted rescuing, there could be the devil to pay.

For that matter, there might be the devil to pay here, too, in the currency of the realm.

She sat down in the depleted cottage and pondered the situation. So they thought she was a witch. Then she owed it to them, and to herself, to be a good one. That old scarecrow Dorcas seemed to get away with it. She could do the same, if she put her scanty abilities to proper use. If only she'd worked harder in school!

She looked up. There was a scuffling footstep outside, the latch clicked, and Dorcas stood in the doorway. She was the very picture of the wicked old witch, crabbed, bony and all in black. Yet her raddled face wore a meek and deeply humble look, and as soon as she saw Sophie, she sank to the floor in a curtsey, her head lowered to her knee.

Sophie rose up in concern. She had never seen anyone curtsey before.

'What's up?' she said, going over. 'Jet lag?'

Chapter Seven

The Elders' spy had spent some uncomfortable hours pretending to be a scarecrow, a choice of disguise he now regretted. The birds, to begin with, treated him with gross disrespect. And then, owing to the prevalence of casual passers-by, he had been obliged to keep still, with even less mobility than the trees in Cankered Wood, which prevented eavesdropping, as everything happened annoyingly out of earshot.

His vigil was not wholly unrewarded, however. He saw Simon and Sophie enter the barn in a furtive and conspiratorial manner. Shortly afterwards Prudence, the tax collector's daughter who was destined to become a priestess, followed them. Here was a scoop indeed. That girl was suspected of being in league with the witches. He had always thought her too good to be true.

Hardly had Prudence entered the barn when the blonde stranger, Sophie Margaret Oakroyd, left it as if she were striding into battle. Some time afterwards Simon and Prudence came out. The spy could not determine whether they were lovingly entwined or whether Prudence was simply in need of physical support. Seeing Simon's air of relief, visible even at two hundred yards, when he disentangled himself and set her on the road home, he decided that it must be the latter. He noted also that Prudence seemed to recover her strength somewhat when Simon was out of sight, although his trained eye perceived that she walked in an uncertain and pensive manner. But whatever the issue between them, the fact that they had been seen with the ash-blonde witch was news indeed, and should earn him a bonus.

He was preparing to inch his way across the field to shed his disguise in a ditch when a large crow flapped into sight. He looked at it apprehensively. Then he stared, gulped, and stared again. Out of the blue sailed a witch on a broomstick, scarcely higher than the trees. She was making for the Oakroyds' cottage.

'She's got a nerve!' gasped the spy. Of course the arrogance of Dorcas, who was in cahoots with Elders and enchanted princesses, was well-known, but it was pushing her luck a bit far to sail about brazenly like this in broad daylight.

Or had things gone too far already? Was Urstwile done for? Were the Black Powers about to take over? The blonde witch to the south of the town, Dorcas to the north, the Chief Elder adrift in Cankered Wood, the trees hopping around like frogs, and a fifth column inside the town led by a traitor masquerading as a saint?

Resolutely, the spy began walking in the direction of the Oakroyds' cottage. He had taken two steps when blind panic seized him. He turned tail and hurtled across the field, causing a murmuration of starlings, who had been pecking about among the crops and occasionally glancing at him with derision, to burst into the air as if hit by a bomb.

Prudence walked slowly home, too lost in her own sad thoughts to notice the hard looks she was getting.

Even had she noticed them, she wouldn't have cared. She had trained herself to thrive on hard looks. She was a collector's daughter. Tax collectors were hated, and there was a legend in Urstwile that their daughters, like hangmen's, never married. At school the children had barred her from their games. So she had barred them back. She had turned teacher's informant. She took good care to get her sums right, and hand in her essays in time, with the right sentiments in them, so that she couldn't be faulted; and when she left school she took equal care to choose the right career, not teacher's pet now, but God's, so that she could put everyone else in the wrong, and justify herself.

She had talked herself into leading a life without love, which, she had nearly convinced herself, was disgusting. She was the loneliest girl in Urstwile, possibly in the universe. She had no friends and her parents disliked her. Her mother, when asked anything whatever about her, said, 'She must decide for herself; she's old enough now', and pointedly changed the subject. Her father was glad that she was going to be a priestess because it saved him giving her a dowry. He lived in an edifice of his own making, supported on columns of figures.

Yet what Prudence dreamed, at night, alone, would have caused the greatest astonishment. It caused her the greatest guilt, for which she atoned by condemning it in others. She sometimes said, darkly, 'I know what goes on.' And so she did, darkly.

But now Simon had broken up the pattern of her ways. He had hinted that he loved her. Oh but he had: how else could you interpret what he had done and said? But their path was crossed by a wicked witch who had fallen out of the sky into their world.

But, in her heart's core, in her heart of hearts, Prudence

knew that this was not true. It was this knowledge, deep inside, that made her so sad and so bitter. She had seen Sophie, her arms round Simon, her face upturned, and it had been the very tableau of her own most private dreams and longings. She was not truly offended, and she knew it. She just envied and hated the sweetness of it. She felt ugly, and it made her hate Sophie all the more.

So when she had awakened from her swoon and told Simon, 'I know you love me,' it was without complete conviction. The voice in her heart of hearts denied it.

Simon, with the greatest possible tact and politeness, denied it too. He would not so far forget himself as to fall in love with a future priestess. That would be wrong, very wrong. Oh, he was sure she still meant to be a priestess! It was (he reminded her, with inspiration) what God wanted. Oh, she might have doubts, but she had been ill, and illness weakens our resolve, but she must not *dream* of giving up, it would be such a loss to the community! His easy, rather slow way of speaking deserted him and he spoke in urgent squeaks. He kept gulping and darting desperate glances at the barn door. He was clearly frantic to get rid of her and rush after the departing witch. Prudence had deliberately tortured him by prolonging her faintness and making him help her across the field, but it had given her little satisfaction. Oh how she hated Sophie Oakroyd! It was making her feel quite ill.

And also, for the first time in her life, she felt secretly in the wrong. This was intolerable. This made her murderous.

She entered her room, looked with disgust at her made-up face in her glass, and began taking off the new dress, for which she had conceived an intense dislike. As she was pulling it over her head a stone crashed through her window, showering her with glass. Muffled in the dress, she escaped injury. She pulled it off hurriedly and picked her way with nervous haste across the littered floor to the door, which she locked and leaned against, panting. From outside, a swelling chorus of crowd noises assailed her ears. A mob was carrying hard looks a stage further.

'Levitation,' said Sophie. She looked at the broomstick with scientific interest. 'Fascinating. I've seen it done at college. One of our lecturers used to float out of a tenth storey window and in again at another. But you're an advance on him.'

Dorcas had straightened up from her curtsey cautiously, like a boxer getting up off the canvas, and now stood watching Sophie with eyes like crooked pins.

'Flying? You mean my flying?' She screwed up her face in her effort to grasp the mystic words. 'How did you get here, mistress?'

'Er –' said Sophie. She was under strict orders not to impart knowledge of this sort. Besides, how could she explain deatomisation and reassemblage? 'Er – *flew* in, you know.'

'Over the mountains!' said Dorcas, and looked sidelong at the floor. 'There is deep magic!'

'On the floor?'

'Don't mock me, mistress. You flew in on the wings of the great storm that black night.'

'Well, in a manner of speaking. But look,' went on Sophie, in a rather silly, artificial voice, 'I'm not being a good hostess! Is there anything I can do for you?'

Dorcas looked at the young girl before her and was sure that such beauty was more than human. That mirror which used to answer her with, 'Madam thou art the fairest of them all', had been a provincial mediocrity with low standards. She was so consumed with jealousy that she writhed visibly, but she turned the movement into a fawning one, and became a snake charmer.

'Oh mistress,' she croaked piteously, clasping her claw-like hands together, 'I am an old, old woman. Make me young again.'

Sophie stared at the emaciated crone, at a loss. Dorcas misinterpreted her silence and spoke rather more briskly.

'I know you don't want to give away secrets. But you helped Prudence and Reuben without telling them how it was done.'

'It would fill your face out,' ventured Sophie, most rashly, 'if you had some teeth.'

'Teeth!' Dorcas had only one or two spikes. 'Can you even replace them?'

'I know of those who can,' said Sophie reluctantly. They'd go mad back home if they heard her talking like this.

'Ah. Unseen powers.'

'Well, yes.'

Dorcas felt a pang of suspicion. Long years of double dealing had made her a shrewd judge of character, and the uncertainty in Sophie's voice made her doubt the girl's authority. Perhaps she was just a privileged idiot, like the enchanted princesses. Perhaps she came from a world of very advanced magic which she simply took for granted. In that case Dorcas's best course would be to stop being a creep and go back to her attractive first plan of ripping out Sophie's heart and chewing it. But two things happened to prevent her.

The considerate robot had taken the Oakroyds' portable equipment away, but had left the modern fittings of the cottage intact for Sophie's use till her return. Like most old cottages, this one was rather dark, and Sophie at this moment saw fit to switch on the light. The flood of brilliant light from nowhere drew a cry of wonder from the witch. In Urstwile the best houses were just getting used to the newly-invented marvel of the oil-lamp. Dorcas's hand was checked. Not even the elementals could equal this.

The second thing was a clamour from outside, drawing ominously nearer. It was compounded of a blowing of whistles, a banging of tin trays, a hooting of hooters, a tramping of feet, a ragged chorus of shouts, and the high wild screaming of women.

'What's that?' asked Sophie, turning pale.

Dorcas had turned paler still, maggot-white, steamed-cod white. 'We need all your powers now, dearie,' she said. 'It's a witch-hunt.'

Chapter Eight

So far, in his short life, Simon had confined his interests
to agriculture and horses. He had known vaguely that
women were as roses, i.e. apt to fall to pieces, and that
they were uncertain, coy, and hard to please. He had
believed all this indulgently, envisaging no serious
trouble in any dealings with them. Sophie and Prudence,
coming upon him almost simultaneously, were a revelation. He supposed that both were mad, and he was
now wondering whether this was just coincidence or if
the condition was common to the whole female sex.

He sat brooding in the farmhouse kitchen while his
horse, Cuthbert, watched him anxiously through the
open upper half of the door. The poor animal thought
itself responsible for Simon's state, but although it had
the proverbial good sense of its species it was wrong in
this. Simon's unease had two sources. One was the
most irksome of all worries, how to rid himself of someone in love with him whose love he did not return. He
felt a kind of exasperated pity for Prudence, that was
all. If he saw her coming he would take to the hills.
Sophie had stunned him. He could not believe that
anyone as wonderful as she could be so cruel. To be
sure, he believed her innocent, a child of nature, but in
that case she should *act* innocent, she should be dewy-
eyed and wondering, she should be the dream-girl for

whom he'd gladly lose the world; she should *not* be insanely unreasonable like any other girl. He went over the scene in the barn a hundred times. Again and again he washed his hands of her and consigned her to whatever barbarism she had come from, and again and again he was flooded with self-doubt and the dread that he had somehow behaved unworthily. He didn't know what to think. He was in love.

His mind turned to a common male solution: heroic deeds. He pictured himself earning her devotion by saving her from fire, flood or personal outrage. He didn't know that women, while, at the time, appreciating rescue in distress, usually married someone else, as a hero whose deeds are behind him is likely to be a bit flat as a domestic partner. He craved chivalrous action. He fancied killing a dragon, but he had only ever seen one, in the Urstwile zoo, about thirteen centimetres long.

Thinking on these lines, he turned his resentment with Sophie into rage with the world in general. His fuming was interrupted by the sound of wheels in the yard, and he looked out to see a coach drawn by two horses. Tobias, the law-enforcer, got out, followed by three dreadful-looking men, one of whom was Reuben, the blacksmith. Tobias was lean, dark, and sallow-skinned, with a screwed-up face as if he were sucking a lemon. The three thugs lurched after him, holding their arms slightly away from their bodies, as if squeezing things under their armpits.

Tobias said: 'Your name is Simon Goodman?'

'You know quite well what my name is,' said Simon. His sympathy for people with nasty natures did not extend to Tobias. People like Prudence were the victims of their own natures, whereas Tobias revelled in his own nastiness, was religious in it.

'Simon Goodman,' said Tobias, 'I am arresting you on the charge of consorting with witches, and I have to warn you that anything you say may be taken down and used in evidence against you.'

'Then take this down,' said Simon. 'I am not a pig farmer, so there's no place for the likes of you on my farm. Get out.'

The corners of Tobias's mouth turned down, his eyes half-closed, and he made a slight gesture to his three companions. He had picked up this action from some travelling players. Reuben came forward first, his head lowered, his arms dangling so low that his knuckles all but trailed along the ground. Simon slammed the upper half of the door against his face. He then slung open both halves while Reuben was still rocking on his heels and hurtled out, landing him a tremendous punch on the jaw. Reuben fell, as an Urstwile poet would have put it, in a crumpled heap. He had not hit the ground before Simon grabbed the other two men by a shoulder apiece and crashed their heads together, then flung them aside left and right. None of the three moved. The fight had lasted one and threequarter seconds.

Tobias dashed for the coach and scrambled into the driver's seat. But now the horse, Cuthbert, took a hand. He had watched his master's actions with warm approval. The truth was, Cuthbert was embarrassed by his own name. He thought it effeminate. In compensation he dreamed of doing daring things, like a war horse. He charged the coach, ramming it so hard with his massive shoulder that it nearly turned over and its nearside wheel broke off. The two horses bolted, dragging the crippled coach behind them. Cuthbert went over to Tobias, who lay where he had been pitched, and gently held him down with his forefoot, for he abhorred unnecessary violence. It was too late for such solicitude, however. Tobias had broken his neck.

Simon looked soberly at the wreckage. He was a peace loving lad and he was sorry that Tobias and his crew had come upon him in a bad temper. Reuben and his companions were sitting up, groaning and protesting.

'Punching people in the face unexpected!'

'Banging people's heads together!'

'Could fracture their skulls.'

'Could give them brain damage.'

Simon took one look at Tobias, then led Cuthbert to the stable and harnessed him to the cart.

'Get in,' he commanded the three heavies.

'What for?'

'Hospital.'

He carted the corpse and the hangdog trio to the cottage hospital on the south side of the town. He was ready to make a confession, but the priest who ran the hospital had already seen the driverless coach screeching past outside and had run out and halted the horses, and before he could speak had fairly explained to him what had happened to his passengers: they were the victims of an accident. The coach must have hit an obstruction; one wheel was ripped right off. Simon, unswervingly honest, tried to correct them, but the three thugs shouted him down, seizing the priest's explanation eagerly, for they were ashamed to have been beaten in a fight by one young man in a time of one and threequarter seconds. Accident, right. The wheel of the coach had hit a tree. Or boulder, yer. All flung out. Right. Simon had picked them up and brought them here. Yer.

'This could have been serious,' said the priest sternly. 'Those fine horses might have broken their legs. Fortunately they are only frightened. Brother Martin is tending them.'

'Tobias –' said Simon.

'Oh yes,' said the priest, with a brief glance at the body on the bed, 'he's a goner.'

A distant clamour reached Simon's ears. It seemed to come from two directions: from the region of his farm, and from the town itself.

'Witch-hunt,' he said in sudden horror.

There must be two mobs. One would be following Tobias and his crew, seeking trouble with himself. The other . . .

That wilful, headstrong Sophie must have gone into the town in defiance of his warning. Yes, she had been setting out that way when he had stopped her earlier. The mob in the town was attacking her.

Anger and fear rose in his heart, together with a kind of exultation. His chance of a noble deed had come. Cuthbert looked round at him with a kindling eye, and laid back his ears and pawed the ground. He was in this too.

Confined, as a rule, to slow plodding with the plough, Cuthbert set off with thè excitement of a bird let out of a cage, even prancing on his hind legs once or twice; then he was off in a thunderous gallop towards the town, the cart bouncing and creaking behind him. Two dogs from a nearby farm gave chase, and so, shortly, did three pigs, some hens, some geese, and a swarm of bees, who poured from the hive with a whirr like a circular saw. The rout was even joined by a fox, over-joyed to be chasing instead of being chased, who raced along for several hundred yards until pulled out by his vixen, who dragged him back to the lair and spent the afternoon scolding him shrilly and reminding him of his family obligations. Eventually the bees decided that the chase was frivolous and returned to the hive. The geese decided that it was futile and flew off in several directions. The other creatures dropped out exhausted, till the grass verges were strewn with their panting bodies. Cuthbert pounded on into the town.

The roads into it were almost empty. The square in the town centre was a seething mass of people, yelling, jeering, full of righteous indignation, and thoroughly enjoying themselves. For generations the people of Urstwile had led quiet and orderly lives, but the heart of man will never be permanently still; it will break out, as a tamed wolf will suddenly revert to type.

Standing in the cart as it raced down the main thoroughfare, Simon made out a slight, shrouded figure, being dragged in the direction of the pillory. Urstwile tradition maintained that it was advisable to hood a witch when bringing her to justice, lest she should turn the evil eye on her captors. Witch-hunting having long been out of fashion, this mob had failed to find a hood, but had substituted a blanket, which they had thrown over the head and body of their victim and tied about with ropes. Her dress must have been torn off in the struggle, because the sight of her from the waist showed her to be wearing only a petticoat, so that she was dressed with perfect propriety, but not for the public gaze. This enraged Simon still further. He drove into the town square like thunder. Cuthbert's eyes were rolling; flecks of foam flew from his mouth, and his nostrils shone with blood. The crowd scattered in terror and confusion, leaving the poor blinded girl groping pitifully in his path. He swerved past her, pulled up just long enough for Simon to reach out and haul her into the cart, then rushed upon the pillory at the edge of the square. This was by now a mere ornamental antiquity, and a couple of citizens were struggling to unscrew it for use. These also fled before Cuthbert's charge, and he reached it unopposed. He reared up, and with a few tremendous blows of his forefeet, smashed it to firewood.

The Urstwile Civic Guard, meanwhile, had turned out to quell the disturbance, and were forming fours in the background. They were performing this action with great precision: a pace to the rear with the right foot, a pace to the left with the left foot, then bring the right foot smartly up to the left. By the time Cuthbert had demolished the pillory, they had completed the movement to their sergeant's satisfaction, and now formed a square for firing: front rank lying, second rank kneeling, third rank standing, with the fourth ready to replace any casualties. In their haste, they had forgotten to bring their muskets with them, and Simon could see that if he turned back and charged into them, he would cause some serious injury. Besides, the way south seemed fraught with trouble. He therefore galloped out of town in a northerly direction, pursued by a lot of noise and some half-heartedly thrown missiles, and did not halt the cart till it had reached the edge of Cankered Wood.

Now, far from the madding crowd, he set about tenderly unwrapping the squirming bundle on the floor of the wagon.

Then his jaw dropped.

Then he quickly conceded that since no girl, not even Prudence, should be dragged into the street in her petticoat, smothered in a blanket, and stuck in the pillory, his efforts had not been wholly wasted. While Cuthbert stood and steamed, and Prudence modestly pulled the blanket round her and gazed on him with dog-like devotion from among its folds, he looked about him and pondered what to do next. A distant but swelling uproar told him that the mob had got itself together again and was renewing the hunt.

The mob descending on the Oakroyds' cottage, having an old woman and a young girl to tackle, paused warily, and decided to lay siege. This gave Dorcas time to think. She still couldn't make Sophie out. The girl could do wonderful things, like creating light, and yet she seemed uncertain and afraid. Was she really thousands of years old? Or was she as green as she sometimes looked? Or was *that* a cunning act?

'Can't you use your powers on this rabble, mistress?'

'I've left my gear at home,' said Sophie glumly.

'Could you not summon the forces at your disposal?'

Sophie could, of course; a word on the walkie-talkie would fetch robots who would whisk her back to civilisation in no time; but there would be such trouble if she did, both for herself and her father, that life would not be worth living.

'They might not like that.'

'Not much at your disposal, then, are they?' said the witch sourly. She peered out of the window to where a line of citizens lay in hiding, with the inefficient cover of a cat stalking birds. 'Well, I'm not staying till that lot drags me to the stake. I'm going to fly back home, and they can find out what it's like to have an away-match with me. If you're the witch I take you for, you'll come with me. If not, stay here and take your chance.'

'Levitation,' whispered Sophie again, her mouth trembling. She went to the under-the-stairs cupboard and fished out an old birch broom which must have been there for many years.

'I'm Sophie. Fly me,' she murmured.

She quivered with fearful speculation. She was remembering the levitation classes at college, in the grounds with a big safety-net. 'Your body *does not exist,*' the lecturer would insist. 'Your *mind is all*, and it will take you where it wills.' And he would float horizontal up to the level of the gymnasium roof to glide gracefully back to the field. Then the revoltingly goody-goody Orestilla sisters, Fenella, Prunella, and Estella, would float in arrowhead formation over the net and sink down on to it for his approval, fat, smug creatures whose bodies existed in too great quantity for Sophie's liking. Then her turn would come, and she would flop about in a most incompetent fashion. 'You are not *willing yourself* to rise, Sophie,' the lecturer would say with strained patience. 'You are not *wishing* it.'

'I like it better on the ground, actually.'

Sometimes the lecturer would advocate gripping some object, a pole, for instance, to aid concentration. 'You'll have heard the fairy tales about witches flying on broomsticks,' he would say. 'Ah! Don't laugh! Those ignorant old women knew more than you think! Of course, the broomstick itself was nothing, but as an *object of focus* it meant a lot . . .'

Sophie gripped the broomstick handle and set her teeth. Dorcas gave her a curious glance, then scowled and muttered to herself. She, Dorcas, who hated the whole of nature, had momentarily caught herself liking this girl. For a witch, such a feeling was very bad. She glared at Sophie as evilly as she could.

'Can't wait all day!'

'I can't go just like this!'

'So what are you going to do, take a suitcase?'

'Will they really burn us?'

'Want to stay here and see?'

It was like being required to swim an ocean when you have never managed more than a floundering length at the baths, but needs must, thought Sophie, when the devil drives. At the back of the cottage was a small, walled garden where they would be unobserved by their besiegers, and, feeling weak and faint, she led Dorcas out into it. The witch straddled her broomstick and became one with it, pulling the handle up almost vertical. Sophie fumbled clumsily with the awkward folds of the Urstwile skirts. Once more, Dorcas gave her that wry, half-sympathetic glance.

'Sit right back. Sit against the tail.'

'It isn't a squirrel, you know,' said Sophie faintly. But Dorcas gave no more advice; she was away with a *whoosh*! like a rocket; a shout of rage and terror went up from the mob; and the next moment she was a mere speck in the sky.

'It is simply a matter of *falling upwards*,' Sophie heard the lecturer insisting. 'It is as easy as falling downwards. The law of gravitation has *long* been disproved as a *mathematician's myth*. No: *upwards*, Sophie.'

Sophie hauled the handle up as Dorcas had done. The faces of several besiegers appeared over the garden wall, staring hatefully, like cats at a grounded bird. But the broom seemed to be as firmly fixed to the ground as Prudence's hammer had been.

Prudence's hammer. That was it. 'Get up, Prudence,' she had said, and Prudence had got up. Suddenly she became perfectly calm and full of will. 'Get up, Sophie,' she said, with cool authority. 'Lift up your heart and fly.' And, as some bolder spirits began clambering over the wall, carrying pitchforks and grappling-irons, she became a glittering streak skywards, moving so fast that she left a whiplash of white vapour behind her.

At three or four hundred yards, having pulled the handle back too far, she looped the loop, and when she tried to straighten out, the broom end swung up, and she hung in the air like an exclamation mark. Having persuaded herself that she was weightless, however, she had limitless strength. With a mighty heave she swung the broom down, vaulted on to it, and got on course again. Gripping convulsively, she pursued the distant speck of Dorcas, who was now high above the town travelling north. Sophie's skirts flapped and crackled in rapid staccato bursts. A skylark, rehearsing before evensong, sat back on the air, flabbergasted, its claws stuck out and its wings awry, like a tiny parcel blown undone. 'Hail to thee, blithe parcel!' called Sophie, but her words were lost in the wind. She felt even lighter in the head than she did in the body. She felt drunk. She thought of the smug Orestilla sisters and their puny practice flights, and laughed with scorn. 'Fenella and Prunella and Estella,' she chanted deliriously to herself, 'Creep in this petty pace from day to day . . .' She felt mad. It was wonderful.

The town was a toy cluster below her, and far to the west of it she could see the castles of Urstwile's obsolete aristocracy, the barons and earls and princesses who lived on what the rest of the population was willing to pay for tradition. Now she was over Cankered Wood, the tree tops so close that they heaved like a sea. Terrified, she wondered wherever she could land. But Dorcas was near now, turning in ever-descending circles, and Sophie, manoeuvring the broom in tense and painstaking imitation of her, followed this downward spiral, until, on fire from the wind, exhilarated, giddy, exhausted, she dropped to rest before Dorcas's house, sprawled on the earth, and examined her blistered hands.

Now all exhilaration died. If she had felt like a rocket, she was now the fallen stick. She was here with nothing but what she was wearing. She had surely lost Simon for ever. She was branded as a witch. She could never leave this ghastly place. The hovel was filthy. Its gruesome owner leered at her from the doorway.

Dorcas contemplated her. No-one but herself and the cat had ever been inside the hovel. But no-one else had ever dropped in like this.

The cat seemed to be thinking on the same lines. It approached Sophie, sniffed her, nose to nose, with great delicacy, and then walked purposefully to the door, where it said miaow in one syllable.

Dorcas grinned, showing her long eye teeth. She ducked under the dangling corpse of a ferret and opened the door.

'Come on,' she said. 'Walk into my parlour.'

Chapter Nine

This, thought Simon in deep disillusionment, is what real life does to high romance: it turns it into farce. What knight of legend had ever rescued the wrong girl?

Well, he had made a proper mess of things. That other mob must have reached the Oakroyds' cottage by now and were probably lynching them. Should he rage back the way he had come and try rescuing the right girl this time? No, he couldn't hope to take everyone by surprise again. The mob in the town were looking for him, the Civic Guard had probably remembered their muskets, and Cuthbert was tired. Besides, there was Prudence to consider.

He looked grimly at her as she huddled in the cart, blanket-enfolded and submissive. By what ludicrous blunder had she got into this? Had the mob collared the wrong girl too? Would they have apologised and let her go? Unless she herself had deliberately gone out into the streets in her petticoat with a blanket over her head, no. They must have known who she was. And they were going to stand a future priestess in the pillory? Were all the people mad? Anyway, he couldn't put her at risk again.

'We shall have to hide in the wood.'

Prudence poked a hooded and fearstruck face over the side of the cart. 'But it's the *haunted* wood!'

'Plenty of people enter it,' said Simon darkly.

'But they're *wicked* people! I'm good!'

'Can you make the mob believe that?'

He fetched Cuthbert, who had been released from the cart and was cropping the grass at the edge of the wood. He made a stirrup with his hands and hoisted Prudence on to the horse's back. She rode his bare back in side-saddle position, alternately clutching at his mane and the blanket, and ducking fearfully, as they entered the wood, to avoid being scalped.

She, too, knew that things had gone badly wrong. Even if the citizens lost their wish to lynch her (which she thought irrational) her reputation was now ruined. Her joy at being rescued by Simon had faded. His grim resignation told her that she was the last person on earth with whom he wanted to be lost in a wood. Her heart's desire had been to be with him for ever. What a swindle it was to get your heart's desire! Perhaps this was her punishment for sinfully wanting him. Perhaps she was doomed to wander for ever in this horrible place with a man who loathed her.

'We can't stay here, Simon,' she said plaintively.

'No alternative.'

'But what shall we eat?'

'Roots and berries.'

The only roots were tree-roots, black and hard as iron, and the only berries were evil dark-green beads so obviously poisonous that just looking at them gave you colic, but she was cowed by his brusque sarcasm and did not argue.

'What about if it rains?' she asked forlornly.

'We shall make a rude shelter out of the branches.'

The branches here would be about as suitable as barbed wire for a shelter, however rude, but still she didn't protest. She was afraid of him in this mood.

Now, as Cuthbert took his first slow steps into the wood, the noise of the advancing mob grew stronger. This mob scorned taking its quarry by surprise. It banged trays, blew whistles, yelled and chanted slogans.

'The Civic Guard should stop them!' said Prudence indignantly. The kettle drums of the Civic Guard could indeed be heard, but they seemed to be marshalling the mob rather than stopping them, as they sometimes marshalled processions at festivals.

Simon intended not to call on Dorcas's hovel, but to use it as a landmark. Keep that in view, and they'd always find their way back. Its crooked chimney was just visible from here. The path to it, trampled by many feet over the years, was wide and short. And yet, having gone a little distance along it, he was taken aback to find a tree in his way. It was a huge gnarled tree and it completely blocked the path. Simon had never believed the superstition that the trees in this wood could move. The roots of a tree were as deep in the earth as its height above it, and for them all to be zigzagging about would create an earthquake! But the fact remained, the tree had got in the way, or else the path unexpectedly twisted. He turned Cuthbert to where an opening of some sort presented itself, and Prudence cowered down as some long stems clawed at her hair. Three steps more, and there were trees everywhere, a tangled opacity of trees. Simon led Cuthbert through the widest gap he could find, horse and girl getting scraped in the process; but now they found themselves in a small glade like an arboreal cell, from which there seemed to be no exit at all. They were shut off from all sight of the hovel now, and from everything else, except, in dingy splashes through the overhead enlacement, the sky.

'It's getting dark,' said Prudence wanly.

'It's the shade of the trees,' said Simon curtly.

'I can see the stars.'

So could he; it was getting dark, and chilly too.

There were gaps between the trees where a man could pass, but none wide enough to let Cuthbert through.

'I'll investigate,' said Simon.

'Don't leave me!' cried Prudence in terror, and slipped to the ground, hurting her feet, for she was only wearing bedroom slippers.

'I'm only going a few steps,' he said impatiently.

'*Please* let me come with you!'

He shrugged and worked his way through the nearest gap, with Prudence wincing and whimpering after him. He took his few steps with her clinging to his arm. It was now quite dark. The trees were so dense that they could hardly move.

He groped irresolutely about. Sick, sick at the heart was he. Prudence's snivelling exacerbated him. It occurred to him that here would be an ideal place to murder her. She would never be found. How near are we to actual murder when we commit it in fantasy? In Simon's case, not very near. He was almost immediately ashamed of the thought of harming this poor, frail, frightened creature, and for the first time that day he showed some tenderness towards her.

'Don't worry, lass.' He put his arm about her, awkwardly. 'We're not done for yet.'

But now, to the rustling, the scuffling, the squeaking, and all the other animal noises usually heard in a wood at night, was added another sound: a thin, rare, desolate moaning. Its utter despair chilled the blood.

'What's that?' said Simon hoarsely.

Prudence, clinging to him with both arms, said tragically: 'It's the crying of the night ones.'

'Who are they?'

'The ones who have never got out of this wood alive!'

Cuthbert, left alone, looked about him. Whereas he too had been hopelessly lost when with Simon and Prudence, he could now see his way quite clearly. They had strayed from the path, but a drifting moon showed him the way back to it, and nothing got in his way. A weak light glimmered from the hovel. He could not see what all the fuss had been about. At every few paces the intelligent beast neighed loudly to guide his master back to him. He had a snickering sort of neigh, rather effeminate for so large a brute.

Sophie followed Dorcas into the hovel in a state of deepest depression, and found that she had stepped into a collector's dream.

'Oh!! It's *lovely*!'

The suits of armour on either side of the great inglenook fireplace! The spinning wheel, the polescreen, the wooden cradle filled with dried flowers! The dark, solid furniture, including one magnificent chest with a blaze of brass ornaments on it! The low oak beams! The decorative plates (with handpainted flowers) on the walls! The cabinets full of silver!

'Glad you approve,' said Dorcas, quite benignly. She was used to shutting her door behind her and gloating over her treasures like a miser. It was gratifying for someone else to admire them.

'All this would be worth a *fortune* where I come from,' said Sophie.

'It's worth quite a bit here. It comes from the stately homes of Urstwile, most of it.'

'It's beautiful.'

Once again, Dorcas was disturbed by a pang of liking for this girl. She said some very pretty things in that sweet, fresh young voice of hers. Then she became angry with herself. This would never do. Her long, outcast existence had been dedicated to hating life in all its forms, and here she was growing soppy over a silly child.

Or was she such a child? Or a superwitch, with this innocent look her final triumph?

Dorcas went into the kitchen and concealed a wicked knife about her person. It would put an end to all this speculation if she chopped the girl to pieces here and now. Bad, if she were making the wrong move, though. At her age, she didn't want to be turned into a toad or a nasty little lizard. She opened the kitchen door a trifle and scowled into the trees. Dusk was beginning to fall.

'Come, my little spirit, sitting in a foggy cloud,' she said, resuming her witch's croak. 'Give me a sign? Is she all-powerful? Or is she fit only to make cat's meat?'

She went back with slow ominous steps, plonk, plonk, plonk, and stood in the doorway, and thereupon she received the sign she had asked for. A 'bleep, bleep' came from the region of Sophie's bosom, a tiny squeak as if from a faint-hearted field mouse. Sophie unhooked her pendant, stuck the ends in her ears, and began talking to the instruments of darkness. Dorcas was awed. All she could hear from the mystic apparatus was a faint 'squarkle-squarkle', but Sophie clearly made sense of it, and was answering with lucid if mysterious words.

The instrument of darkness was Sophie's father.

'I can't find my brown shirt with the button-down collar.'

'Airing cupboard.'

'*Air*ing cupboard? I've been searching the *ward*robe.'

'No, airing cupboard. How are you managing without me?'

76

'Well, *cop*ing,' came her father's voice, rather aggrieved. Then, reluctantly, 'What about you? You're *all right*, I suppose?'

It depends what you call all right, thought Sophie. The sensible thing would be to demand immediate help. But she was clinging to the feeble hope of seeing Simon again.

'Sophie?'

'I'm all right.'

'I mean, I *could* send for you immediately, but –'

'I'm all right.'

'I mean, unwise to *press* them to return you . . . It's the elections, you see,' said the professor, with a timely recollection. 'They're very near. If we do anything out of order the Neo-Radicals will *seize* on it –'

'Yes, I see,' said Sophie; but she had no interest in politics, and had no idea what the Neo-Radicals wanted, or why it was so wrong.

'Luckily, you're in about the safest place on earth.'

'Yes.'

'*Air*ing cupboard, you say?'

Sophie replaced her pendant while Dorcas looked at her reverently.

'You were talking to your masters.'

'That particular master,' said Sophie, 'is lost without me.'

'Ah!' said Dorcas, much impressed.

She went back to the kitchen and returned with some scones and a steaming pot.

'This beverage,' she said humbly, 'is made from rare herbs from a foreign clime. Would you care to try it? You may mix milk with it, or lemon, if you wish. It was a gift from the gentry.'

'I'd love to.'

They sat sipping the beverage, which cheered, but

did not inebriate, while the cat lapped milk on the hearth. Dorcas was chastened. You had to go careful with this one. She was full of surprises and strange words.

The cat pricked up its ears.

'Is that the witch-hunt?' asked Sophie apprehensively, having also heard the distant noises. 'Have they followed us?'

'They'll never get to us. I've enchanted the trees. Don't worry, this wood is full of noises, but when folks lose themselves here, they stay lost, and don't they moan about it!'

'It sounds like the neighing of a horse,' said Sophie.

Chapter Ten

The mob that had besieged the Oakroyds' cottage decided prudently not to break into it, for fear of witchly booby-traps, and returned to the town with the exciting news that the spy had been right, Dorcas *had* flown on a broomstick, and so had the ash-blonde witch, who had even had the impudence to perform some stunts in mid-air.

The mob that had attacked Prudence was quickly restored to order. They were squeamish about entering Cankered Wood, and their protest meeting at the edge of it was marred by the Civic Guard, who kept circling round them banging kettle-drums. A few fines were imposed for depositing litter and suchlike offences.

What finally discouraged them was the reaction of Prudence's father to the state of his house. He returned home tired out after extorting the last few coins from poverty-stricken widows in the suburbs, to find his front lawn trampled, his front door smashed in, muddy footprints on the stairs, a window broken, a bedroom door forced open, and a blanket missing from the bed. In addition to the blanket, his daughter had been taken. His wife had been on the premises but was no use as a witness, having been out at the back, sleeping within her orchard (her custom always in the afternoon).

The tax collector readily turned the situation to his

advantage, as he always did: At first he thought only of demanding compensation for the damage, the loss of his daughter being an incidental piece of good fortune. But then he noted that Prudence had been carried off by Simon to the edge of Cankered Wood. In fact the two of them had *entered* the wood! In fact they must have *spent the night there*! – Simon in shirtsleeves and the girl (he lowered his eyes, for he was a man of high moral standards) in her petticoat. Here was a stroke of luck indeed. Simon would have to marry her. In fact, he might even want to . . . Young Simon Goodman was a comfortable farmer. He supplied most of the town with his produce. For Prudence to marry him would be a much more profitable arrangement than to become a priestess . . .

The tax collector protested so bitterly to the somewhat bewildered Elders that real tears stood in his eyes. There was a disgraceful rumour that his daughter was involved with witchcraft. Didn't they know that she was its sternest foe? Hadn't she proved as much already? It was the people, so depraved as to drag a young girl into the streets improperly dressed, who were guilty of the witchcraft. Yes, they were bewitched! The hag Dorcas had put a spell on them out of revenge for Prudence's recent brave challenge! The hag Dorcas, assisted by that evil creature from the riven oak!

Only Simon, worthy young man, had stood up for her. Oh yes, of course, he was in love with her – their attachment had been an open secret in the family for a long time. But, poor young man, look at the shame he had been forced to! Not to mention Prudence! *and* her devoted parents! The least the Elders could do would be to finance their wedding ceremony at the town's expense, extracted from the erring citizens in the form of taxes!

The wind was taken out of the sails of the erring citizens, and the money from their pockets. To suspect Prudence of witchcraft had been, they now admitted, very far-fetched. They went about looking sorry for themselves as though on the morning after a party.

So, unknown to Simon and Prudence, who thought they were still hunted, things returned to sheepish normal in a sadder and wiser town.

And yet, in various little ways, changes began to make themselves apparent in Urstwile life. Take the case of the poet Gabriel. He found that he could no longer write serious poetry. Inspiration had dried up. He turned his hand to writing advertisements. Here, for example, is one he wrote for Raymond, the shoe-maker:

> *Now I behold Old Sol's refulgent ray*
> *Distinctly through my shoe, its various holes,*
> *I must repair to town without delay*
> *To get some of old Ray's refulgent soles . . .*

It showed some literary skill, but it wasn't commercial.

It was pitch black in the wood now. Pointless, to grope from one entanglement to another. Besides, they might meet the owner of one of those dreadful, moaning voices, and even Simon's brave spirit quailed at that.

'We'll stay here till it grows light.'

The ground was knobbly and spiky and gave off cold as ashes give off heat. Simon was used to working out of doors in all weathers, but to lie here motionless in his shirtsleeves was an ordeal even for him, and he wondered if he would freeze stiff like some hibernating creature. He could hear the staccato rattling of Prudence's teeth.

'I'm c-cold,' she protested.

'Do some physical jerks.'

'I c-can't do ph-physical jerks all night long!'

She lay shuddering, partly with sobs and partly with cold. After a while her misery became more than he could bear, and so did the temperature. He went over to her, lifted the blanket, and lay beside her. She clutched the heavy bicep of his left arm with both hands, as she was wont to clutch her teddy bear at home. For a long time he did not move. At last he slipped his arm under her neck, taking care not to tug her hair, and drew her close to him. She was as cold as a slab of cod, as if there were no warm blood left in her, but she thawed by degrees, and under the cover of night he found her nearness agreeable. He turned, put his other arm round her, and pretended that she was Sophie.

Sophie was finding Dorcas's cottage full of surprises. It even had a bathroom, or rather, a room with a bath in it, not plumbed in – a resplendent hip bath with a ducal crest at one end and a coronet, embossed and gilded, at the other, with a motto on a scroll underneath. There was no plug hole, and when you had emptied it as much as possible with pails and jugs you mopped up the remaining water with a sponge. The water was heated in a copper and carried upstairs in pails. You bathed by the light of an oil lamp.

Dorcas also had cupboards full of dresses, exquisite creations in silk and satin. She changed out of her witch's uniform and wore one at dinner, and became a grand lady. The dinner was a pie of some unknown meat, and was quite the best Sophie had ever tasted. Dorcas lent her a dress, because her own was rather rumpled by now. The inside seams were rather scratchy, and brought home to her the efficacy of Urstwilean underwear, but she would have suffered more than this willingly for the sake of fashion. She loved dressing up, enjoyed her meal, and, within this delicious cocoon of a cottage, had almost forgotten the horrible wood outside.

Dorcas had laid the kitchen knife aside and was permitting herself to sink further and further into liking her visitor. Having spent countless years in the company only of satanic black cats, she found Sophie's delight in her cottage, and her admiration for her taste, very pleasant indeed. Sophie was a new kind of witch. She had class. They could get on very nicely together. They could be partners.

They sat by the log fire, on either side of the fireplace, pleased with themselves and each other's mood. Dorcas looked much less of a hag, partly because of the dress, partly because of the mellow light of the lamp, but mainly because her face had taken on a most unusual expression, a grandmotherly, almost benevolent look.

'Why did you become a witch, Dorcas?'

'I didn't fit in with Urstwile society.'

'Why not?'

'I wrote poetry.'

'Was that a crime?'

'Girls weren't supposed to write poetry.'

'In my country, most of the poetry is written by computers,' mused Sophie. 'Was yours good?'

'Very good.'

'But surely they didn't drive you out because of it, did they?'

'Not exactly, but they thought I was an odd, eccentric girl that no-one would marry. And I didn't want to marry –'

'In my country, there are no more marriages,' said Sophie uncertainly.

'I couldn't see myself cooking meals and sewing

buttons on for half-wits. I had a lot of lovers, and that made me a bad girl. My lovers expected me to be bad, it was part of the attraction, so I said to myself, right, gentlemen, you shall get what you're asking for, and I began studying witchcraft. In an off-hand way, you know, at first. But I learned very quickly. I can learn anything I want to. I'm clever, you know,' said Dorcas simply.

'Yes, you are. How do you make trees move around?'

Dorcas gave her a long, interrogative stare. 'You really don't know? It surprises me, what you do and don't know. One thing's for sure, you'll understand that these things can *never* be explained. M'm? But look. You've stood on a bridge over a stream and watched the water until it has seemed that the bridge is moving and the water is still? Yes? You've done that? You begin to get the idea?'

'Well, no. Only vaguely. But it's very interesting.'

Dorcas's tongue was loosened and she talked at length, discussing such matters as spells and curses and how to make gold. Mixed into a mish-mash of mumbo-jumbo and fakery, thought Sophie, there was a lot of sound psychological knowledge. Dorcas was quite brilliant. She was a natural. Back home, she could be a professor of levitation. But it was too early to point out to her what was science and what was superstition.

'Of course,' said Dorcas, as if reading her thoughts, 'there's a lot of bluff involved. Tricks of the trade.'

'Are you ever sorry you didn't get married, Dorcas?'

'That would have involved far too much bluff.'

Sophie mused. She was not sure that the obsolete slavery of marriage might not be preferable to the life at home, where you had to keep on proving yourself, keep on achieving, achieving, with no excuses if you failed, where the Orestilla sisters did everything right and you did it wrong, where you fell downwards instead of upwards . . . Mightn't it be nice just to give in, dissolve, forsake the individuality they all thought mattered so much, and become a Little Woman, cooking meals for Simon, and sewing buttons on for him, and letting him look after all her needs? In the subdued light of the inglenook, she blushed; these were scandalous thoughts. Yet, what the hell? With a father like hers, she was halfway to living that kind of life already, with none of its compensations.

'You can't do it with animals,' said Dorcas.

'Sorry. What?'

'You can't make them think the trees are moving. Cats. Dogs. Horses. They're never taken in.'

'I was sure I heard a horse neighing.'

'There's nothing you *don't* hear if you stay here long enough. Mind you, when you're working these tricks, you have to keep on the watch for the spirits. They'll get in on your act if they feel like it. They did when the Chief Elder was here a few days ago. They started moving the trees. It gave me quite a turn.'

What a mixture she is, thought Sophie. Part deep understanding, part rubbish. However shall separate these?

'Would you care for some more of the beverage made from rare herbs?' asked Dorcas politely. 'I myself enjoy one after a meal of hedgehog pie.'

'Hedgehog . . . ! Was that what it was?'

'I hope you liked it?'

'Oh! . . . Oh yes, yes, very much . . . Yes, I'd *love* a beverage made from rare herbs, please . . .'

Dorcas's little spirit, sitting in a foggy cloud, was for nearly all the time cold, damp and lonely. Don't waste any sympathy on it; it was a hideous little bat you couldn't take anywhere. But Dorcas, seasoned in her trade, rarely called on it, so that whenever she did so it became wildly excited, and jumped up and down, and flapped its wings, and clucked and hooted and whistled and yelped.

In its shady world the bush telegraph was of tremendous potency, and in no time its agitation became known to the dark underworld masters of things. They had been watching the behaviour of the oafish gang of minor demons they had put out to deep field in Cankered Wood, and very displeased with them they were.

The elation of the little spirit aroused their interest. Perhaps it meant nothing. On the other hand, no smoke without fire. Better look into it.

They despatched a slightly superior fiend to take stock of things.

It was daylight, and the trees were no longer moving, and seemed now to be somewhat wider apart. Slowly and sadly, Simon and Prudence picked their way through them, avoiding each other's eyes. Since awakening, neither had spoken a word.

With every step, he was expecting an outpouring. He was waiting, defenceless, for her to make her demand of him, to take advantage of having been taken advantage of. But she said nothing. Her face was curiously set, as if masking some deep private decision. When at last she did speak, it was quietly, matter-of-fact:

'I'm hungry.'

'Yes,' he said. They had been without food for many hours. 'Yes. We'll get back to my farm somehow. There's plenty to eat there. We'll find Cuthbert and the cart and we'll ride back.'

'I'm not going back.'

'Don't worry, we can skirt right round the town. No-one will see us.'

'You go. I'm staying here.'

'You can't. You'll die,' he said harshly.

'I shall go to Dorcas.'

'You can't, you can't do that.'

'She likes bad people.'

'Prudence –' said Simon, pained.

'I can't be a priestess now. I'm not qualified, not any more. What's the alternative, would you say?'

He gathered up all his courage and began: 'Prudence –'

'Don't say it.'

'There's something that must be said.'

'I don't want to hear it.'

Nothing she could have said could have so disarmed him. She was offering him an unconditional release, yet he racked his wits to make her change her mind. But at this point Cuthbert put his head through the trees. Having failed to summon them the night before, he had stood still all night and dozed, being not more than twenty strides from where they were lying. Simon ran to him, overcome with relief, and examined him anxiously for any signs of ill effects. There were none; and once more, with redoubled urgency, he begged Prudence to ride back to the farm with him.

'You go.'

'If you insist on going to the witch,' he said, 'I'm coming with you.'

He began leading Cuthbert, or rather, he held the bridle while the horse led him. Prudence, with a small gesture of resignation, followed. They made a dismal trek through the wood, depleted, filled with a sense of loss. That is, the two human beings did. The horse was disappointed – now that he'd found them they might be a bit more cheerful about it – but he was philosophical, being used by now to·the extraordinary ways of man.

A zigzag route, some ducking under branches and some squeezing through gaps, and they came at last to the squalid hovel, with the hell broth still slowly erupting noisome bubbles, and the withered corpses dangling about the porch. Prudence, who had shown great fortitude so far, was beaten by this small detail.

'I can't stand dead things,' she said weakly.

'I'll knock.' Simon was glad to have command for the moment.

He led her and the horse to where the foliage hid the porch from view, because the very sight of it had her on the brink of fainting, and, squaring his shoulders, frowning manfully, he strode towards the horrible front door.

At that very moment the door opened and Sophie came out into the sunlight, ducking under the swinging body of a stoat. She was wearing a beautiful flowered dress; her hair was loose about her shoulders and glistened in the sun; she was smiling happily. When she saw him she gave a cry of joy and ran to him with outstretched arms.

'*Simon*!'

He became rigid. He said in a tight voice, 'I did not expect to find you here.'

She did not realise yet how angry he was.

'No, it's a small world, isn't it?' she said cheerfully. 'But do come in! Here you are among fiends!'

Chapter Eleven

Simon was terse and scathing. All Urstwile had known her to be a witch. He alone had stood up for her. Silly of him, wasn't it? Well, at least she'd sunk to her own evil level, this vile shack –

'Wait till you see inside,' said Sophie placidly. 'And don't insult my friend. She's been very good to me.'

'Birds of a feather,' he said bitterly.

'Simon,' said Sophie, still patiently, 'things are not what they seem –'

But now Prudence, deciding that it was taking Simon a long time to knock at a door, showed herself. The self she showed was a crumpled ruin. Traces of her make-up still stuck like scabs to her white, creased face. Her hair hung down, cluttered with leaves and mud. She was wrapped in a grubby blanket, with the torn frill of a petticoat showing. Mud-soaked slippers flopped on her feet. She drooped so forlornly that she looked as if she were hanging from a hook.

'Oh, *really*!' exclaimed Sophie, no longer patient. 'Just got up, has she? Not even dressed? This is a bird of *your* feather, is it?'

He replied sombrely, in much the same words as her own, 'Things are not what you think they are.' His conscience pricked him and he corrected himself. 'At least, not altogether –'

'Let's hope not.' Sophie eyed Prudence again and was touched in spite of herself. Never had she seen anyone look so wretched and defeated. 'I think we'd both better explain.'

Dorcas, who had been cooking breakfast, appeared in the doorway. She had hastily thrown off an elegant morning-coat and put on her witch's gown, and had jammed her pointed hat over her ears, but the effect was spoiled by a pair of blue satin slippers instead of the spiteful boots she usually wore. She adjusted her features to their habitual sinister glare. She eyed the three young people and saw them dismayed and vulnerable, and to her horror she felt a pang of sympathy for them. She had a dreadful misgiving that perhaps she had been on the wrong track all her life. She was clever and adaptable; she could fake any rôle with ease; had she, all her life, been faking the rôle of a witch? Was she to learn this *now*?

She said in a gravelly voice, 'Fair worn out, young master? Hungry, too, I'll be bound.'

Simon said disdainfully, 'Not for any food of yours.'

It cost him an effort to say this. He could smell bacon frying. The sizzle made his mouth water. He pictured gammon rashers spread with eggs. There was an aroma of baking bread.

'That one,' said Dorcas, jerking her thumb at the wilting Prudence, 'looks done in. But if it's against your principles to let her eat, go on, drag her through the woods till she dies, it's no concern of mine.'

'She needs clothing, too,' said Sophie, with a slight sniff.

Simon looked at Prudence and hesitated.

'Well, make up your mind,' said Dorcas.

He said frostily, 'I have no money with me, but you shall be paid. Be so good as to bring some food out to us.'

'I'm not a waitress, young man. If you're going to be my guest, come in.'

Doubtfully, he led Prudence to the door. She required leading; she muffled her head in the blanket as she neared the corpses. Dorcas eyed the young couple sardonically.

'Open house now,' she said, in exaggeratedly sarcastic tones. 'Dorcas the Hospitable. Feeding the hungry and clothing the naked. (Well, the half-naked.) What am I coming to?'

What a shock, the inside of the hovel! And the food! There *were* gammon rashers, any number, it seemed; and fried eggs, and mushrooms, and savoury dropscones, and a scaffolding of bread and butter, all washed down with a singular beverage made from rare herbs, of which he was wary at first, in case it drugged him, but which he soon took to, and drank with milk from a large mug. Dorcas snarled as she served them, telling them to take things or leave them, and that they were not to suppose that she made a habit of feeding passing beggars. Simon was not taken in. He put this change in her down to Sophie's influence. Cold or hot in his feelings for Sophie, he felt progressively hotter as he ate the good food, and he made up his mind that she was here as a kind of missionary. Yes, she had braved this hideous wood alone, and had won over Urstwile's grimmest hag with the sheer power of her innocence! His heart melted as he looked at her. He forgot that she could hardly have furnished the cottage throughout, and endowed it with all its charms, in a single visit. He thought she was wonderful. As he ate he grew mellower still.

Prudence, who had thought she was hungry, had lost her appetite. She nibbled at her food apathetically. She watched Simon's face as he gazed at Sophie.

91

Now and again she looked away as if it hurt her to look any more.

'And you,' said Dorcas raspingly to her, 'if you've stopped picking at that meal, you'd better have a wash and make yourself decent. Come on, I'll find you something to wear.' She turned on Simon with a snarl. 'And don't think you can pay me for what I give her. It'll be worth more than you make in a year.' She turned back to Prudence. 'Come on, then. Lost the power of your legs?'

The eyes that looked up at her were glassy. Prudence stood up. Then Prudence fell down. It was not the dainty collapse she had effected in the barn; she fell flat on her face with a crash. Simon and Sophie knelt by her in concern. Dorcas looked on, her face working with strange emotions.

'Get her upstairs,' she said.

Then she said, 'So we're a hospital now, are we? What next?'

Sophie had slept on a couch, but they put Prudence to bed in the tiny second bedroom. Not surprisingly, there was no bed in it, as Dorcas never entertained, but she had a spare mattress and a number of blankets, all with crests embroidered on them, and a makeshift pallet was made up for Prudence on the floor.

'Can you use your powers to make her better?' asked Simon humbly.

'Me? I'll try,' said Sophie doubtfully. She had learned elementary hypnotism at school, of course. Would that help? Prudence was beyond the aid of hypnotism at present, being apparently in a coma. Like the Sleeping Beauty, thought Sophie, although a sorry beauty just now. Awaiting the prince's kiss? Sophie frowned.

'How did she get here, in this state?'

When he had told her, stammering, she laughed with relief.

'Oh, Simon! So you collected the wrong bundle! I'm so glad! I wish I'd been your bundle!'

'You have understood . . . *all* I have told you?'

'About sleeping with her, you mean? Yes, of course, what is there to understand?'

She did, to her surprise, feel a small pang of dismay over this, but she did not show it. All things are pure to her, thought Simon. She is an innocent child of nature. It was a most comforting reflection, because it allowed him to forgive himself.

'I think your horse comes out best in all this,' she remarked, going outside to inspect Cuthbert, who was fed and watered and statuesque and indifferent to the scenery. 'Isn't he lovely? But why did you call him Cuthbert?'

'From motives of affection,' said Simon gravely.

'I think it's rather soppy. I think you should call him Ebony.'

'He's not black. More charcoal grey.'

'So is ebony, if you burn it long enough.'

Now she told him her story, and his face clouded again.

'*Flew*? But that's witchcraft.'

'No, Simon. Science.'

To leave the wood was out of the question, for three of them were sure that mobs were lying in wait to lynch them, and their fourth member was not fit to be moved. Prudence lay senseless all morning. In the afternoon she began murmuring broken phrases, and Sophie, sitting cross-legged beside her, began tentatively to question her, following up everything she chanced to say. This, she knew, was what the doctors at home did in such cases. Fragment by fragment she pieced together some sort of picture of Prudence's home life. As evening came on the girl lapsed into silence, not asleep but dumb, as if in a deep sulking fit.

'If anyone should be put in that pillory, her parents should,' said Sophie. 'They're *appalling*.'

'Can you cure her?'

'I don't know what's wrong with her. Everything. She really ought to be born again.'

The mysterious things she said fascinated him. Dorcas, who seemed to have come to some conclusions of her own regarding the three of them, left them alone for long periods while she attended to the hell broth for the sake of professional appearances, and the cat gave them a cynical look and walked out too. When they were together in the evening by the inglenook he took her hands and said urgently: 'Sophie.'

'Simon?'

'Let's get out of this together. Take me home with you. Take me to your country.'

'Simon, it wouldn't suit you at all.'

'I'm no city dweller. I'm a farmer. I live with nature. I'd gladly give up civilisation to live with you in your jungle. In a tent. In a cave. Under the open sky. I love you. I'll go anywhere and live any way just to be with you.'

Tears came into her eyes. She was as much in love as he was, but she knew so much more. She was forbidden to describe her country, but what if she tried? Her 'jungle' was a technology-ridden complex he wouldn't begin to fathom, where such love as his would have no chance to exist. She shook her head sadly at him.

'It wouldn't work.'

'Your tribe would reject me?'

She blinked, and two tears rolled down her cheeks. 'You might say that. Yes. My tribe would reject you.'

'Then,' he entreated, 'stay here with me. We'll hide far, far out in the country and let the rest of the world go by.'

'"The rest of the world"!' she repeated, thinking of what that meant. 'I'm afraid it'll catch us up. I'll stay, Simon, till they fetch me.'

'They? I can take you where they'll never find you.'

'I'm afraid you'll never manage that.'

He tried to picture her primitive society. It had uncannily gifted medicine men, perhaps.

'I suppose,' he brooded, 'that your race knows secrets which civilisation has allowed to die out.'

'You're right. My race knows a lot of secrets.'

Dorcas slept in a ducal four-poster, Simon on a couch downstairs, and Sophie on the floor beside her patient, shoulder to shoulder with her, because there was no room to get farther away. Prudence was probably very ill. It was just as well that no Urstwilean doctor could be called, for he would surely have finished her off.

What a mess they were all in! And all because she had chosen to unstick this absurd creature from the pavement! Why hadn't she left well alone? It had been fun, queening it among these simple people and turning their heads, but look at it now! Her father recalled, inflammatory poetry, riots in the streets, lynch mobs, Simon compromised, Prudence ruined!

And the only haven from it all was this cottage, considered the wickedest place in the country!

We do not learn much from our mistakes. Sophie frowned. Dorcas was far superior to the other Urstwileans, and it was sad that she should deceive herself as well as them. For a woman of her ability to make hell-broths and tell clients to spit into the mouths of frogs was quite ridiculous. Surely she should be educated out of such nonsense? Never mind the orders from home.

'Science,' said Dorcas, with great interest. She had forsaken her witch's voice and now sounded like a university lecturer. 'It is a most interesting hypothesis. Most interesting.'

'It stands to reason,' said Sophie, 'there must be a reason for everything. It stands to reason, doesn't it?'

'Psychology,' said Dorcas. 'Mind over matter.' She repeated these words several times over, rather as she was wont to utter her witch's incantations. 'All-in-the-mind,' she intoned.

Simon sat nearby, hearing the technical talk but not taking it in, much as he might have listened to women discussing dressmaking.

'You will appreciate,' said Dorcas apologetically, 'that a lot of what I do is showmanship. It's expected of me.'

'But you have real gifts.'

'Yes . . . Hypnotic persuasion . . . levitation . . . yes, yes . . .' Again she repeated these expressions, rolling them round in her mouth. Science . . . It was a revelation to her. It gave her dignity. She was not only a poet, but a scientist . . . A what? Ah yes: a *psychologist* . . .

'Yet,' she objected, recalling the freak bonfire on the night of the Chief Elder's visit, the dancing trees, and other phenomena, 'inexplicable things sometimes happen.'

'Only inexplicable because you can't explain them, but there must *be* an explanation.'

'Yes, yes,' said Dorcas, deeply impressed.

Hidden behind a log of wood in the fireplace was a black beetle. He was listening intently to this conversation. He was scandalised.

He was not really a black beetle, but the slightly less

minor demon sent by the powers of darkness to inspect Cankered Wood. Having given the oafish demon-gang a severe talking to, and handed them menial tasks to keep them busy, he had turned his attention to the hovel, which he had entered as a black beetle secreted in a fold of Prudence's blanket. The interior of the hovel had greatly shocked him, but nothing like as much as the talk he had just heard.

One thing above all infuriates evil spirits. It is to hear magic and the occult explained away in psychological terms. It undermines their art. It challenges their very existence.

He knew that in many parts of the world this psychological claptrap had taken a hold, but Urstwile was supposed to be free from such corruption. But then, as soon as one's back was turned . . .

He was so agitated that he crawled from behind the log to hear better, and Dorcas spotted him.

'How did that thing get in?' She was exceedingly house-proud. She whipped off a slipper and began to rain blows on the hearth.

Being a spirit, the beetle was unkillable, but one of the conditions of his hateful existence was that he should suffer any amount of pain, and he didn't want to suffer any more than he could help. He took flight, whirring round the room and colliding with the walls. Simon sprang up and began flipping at him with his belt. He found a doorway, zoomed upstairs, planed crazily round Prudence's room and out, nose-dived to the lower floor, and blundered round the room again, until Dorcas threw open the front door, through which he sailed with a high thin whine which faded into the trees.

Prudence sat up screaming.

'Take it away! Aaah! Take it away!'

'There, there,' said Sophie, rather shortly. 'It's gone now. Lie down.'

'A monster with a horrible face!'

'A small insect, dear. Lie down.'

Prudence held her face in her hands and shuddered.

'That smell! That awful smell!'

'There's no smell. Lie down.'

But Dorcas, standing in the doorway, had become rigid. Her thumbs were not so much pricking as stabbing. Her faith in psychology had just taken a jolt fit to kill it at birth. She too had noticed the smell. Emphatically she had. Sulphur.

Chapter Twelve

Professor Oakroyd was worried about his book. It wasn't original enough. What was the good of announcing that the Urstwileans were a charming backward people of docile habits? Everyone knew that. The trouble with being a university professor was that you had to keep inventing discoveries. For example, his colleague the Professor of Literature had just written a book about the cricket jokes in Shakespeare. Now *that* was the kind of thing he needed to do. He needed a gimmick. But what?

He thought of Sophie, still out in Urstwile. She was not very bright. Her mother, who, if his memory served him, had been one of his students, hadn't been very bright either. Nevertheless he had always had a soft spot for the child. He had visited her in the Infant Care Centre quite often, and when she was older, had actually taken her home to live with him. From then on, she had taken care of him. An affectionate little thing. But no capacity for abstract thought.

However, she was still out there, and sometimes simple people hit on valuable data by accident. She might be worth a try. He bleeped her.

Sophie was washing Prudence. She had managed her face and hair and now, in short skirmishes, was washing her body, while Prudence, who was almost too weak to move, tried to conceal herself with corners of the sheet. She believed that Sophie was preparing her for a sacrifice.

'I know why you're doing this.'

'I should think it's obvious.'

'Are you going to drink my blood?'

'Prudence, please don't be disgusting.'

The field-mouse squeak sounded from the pendant. Sophie frowned and swathed Prudence in towels.

'What is it?'

'Ah, Sophie! Sophie, my dear, are you making contact with the natives in any way?'

'I'm in close contact with one now, as it happens.'

'Ah! – you will be prudent, won't you?'

'Completely prudent.'

'Good. I wondered – I wondered: have you come across any *custom* of theirs that you think worth mentioning?'

Sophie thought for a moment. To relate the events of the last two days would ring all the alarms back home and send robots to fetch her within the next half hour.

'Yes,' she said, 'they've discovered tea.'

'*Really*? Are you *sure* of that?'

'Yes. It's very nice. I'll bring you some back.'

'Well, that's really *excellent*. Tell me how you came across this exciting piece of data.'

'I can't just now, I'm busy.'

'In what way?'

'Making contact with natives.'

'I see,' came the Professor's voice doubtfully. He hoped that this merely meant that she was in bed with some young man, but she was rather headstrong and it might be serious. Her information, however, would give his book just the boost it needed. 'Well, tell me as soon as you can. I want to know all about it.'

'All right.'

'About tea, I mean.'

'I know. Bye.'

Prudence could hardly speak for terror. She had misheard the word 'prudent'; she thought her own name had been spoken. The dark forces were discussing her.

'You were talking to the Evil One,' she whispered.

'Oh, that's a bit thick.'

Prudence struggled to sit upright. 'I know what you're doing and why you're doing it.'

'How very clever of you.' Sophie understood Prudence's fears, up to a point, but something perverse in her stopped her from trying to put her mind at rest.

'Dorcas wants her revenge and you want to get rid of me.'

'I don't suppose Dorcas can be bothered,' said Sophie, not without malice, 'but if she does, you can't blame her.'

Prudence fell back on her pillow as if from a blow. She had wanted Dorcas to be hounded, humiliated, burned. Since then she herself had known what it was like to be at the mercy of a mob. She would never forget their feet thundering up the stairs, their smashing in her door, their gloating, jeering faces, the foul hands they had laid upon her, the muffled darkness and the nightmare din as they dragged her through the streets. Never again, never again, would she wish this to happen to anyone, no matter how much of a witch, no matter how wicked.

She said wretchedly, 'I didn't mean it.'

'All right,' said Sophie, more gently. 'Will you please believe that neither of us wants to hurt you? That you're safe here? Will you believe that? Please?'

But Prudence shed tears and looked hopeless.

'Is Simon gone?'

'Yes, Simon's gone.'

Simon, feeling that his manhood demanded it, had left early that morning, not without relief. Dorcas baffled him. Professionally wicked, why did she behave as if she were good, and why was she so ashamed of it? Sophie tormented him. He was even jealous of her care of Prudence. Was it as innocent as it looked, or was she getting at him in some way? As for Prudence, the mere thought of her threw him into such despondency that his mind balked at it, and he busied himself with his horse.

Holding Cuthbert's bridle and allowing himself to be led, he found the way out of the wood so easily that he could not understand why it had ever been so hard. He retrieved his cart and set off, prepared to face whatever trouble lay ahead. He did, however, take the precaution of side-tracking through an Urstwile suburb instead of going through the town centre. The people here watched events from behind curtains rather than forming into mobs.

It so happened that, taking this route, he ran into Prudence's father, the tax collector, who had just wrung the last few pence from a crippled octogenarian. The old man was trying to lift his hands in supplication without falling off his crutches.

'What shall I do for bread, sir?'

'Acorns are a fair substitute, I believe.'

'But sir, how shall I live?'

'The world's big enough, my good fellow. Beg your way through it.'

The collector then noticed Simon, perched behind the reins of the great plough horse.

'My boy! My very dear boy!' He was a man of smooth curves, as if he were made of soap. His face, from brow to chin, could have been drawn with a compass. He had no eyebrows.

'Good morning,' replied his very dear boy, guardedly. He soon learned, however, that he need fear no recriminations from Prudence's father, nor any mob action either. All Urstwile, it seemed, was thrilling to his brave deed, and wanting only to welcome back Prudence, whom they had so sorely wronged.

'They want to prepare a great feast in your honour. No doubt you can guess what they hope to celebrate?'

'No?'

'Aha! I think you can!'

He insisted that Simon should go back with him to his house for lunch. He rode ahead on his dappled mare. As they drew nearer into the town various people greeted Simon, civilly enough, but rather as if they were doing so to order, in the way they cheered officially at public festivals.

The collector's fine house was being renovated at state expense. He was making the most of this, and was having a new kitchen and conservatory installed, all doors and windows repainted, and a new roof.

Observing her parents together, Simon decided that Prudence had survived their upbringing very creditably. Her mother was a sour and bony woman whose face was haggard with suspicion. She looked about her with her eyes, without moving her head. She greeted Simon as cordially as she knew how.

'Very grateful for what you did, Simon,' she said. Her voice was flat and jarring, and without emotion except the fear of being cheated. 'And of course we know that your intentions were entirely honourable, only, of course, not to put too fine a point on it, it does put our Prudence in a compromising position, like, being out two nights running with a young man, and unaccompanied, at that –'

'My dear,' said the collector hastily, 'I'm sure there's no doubt about Simon's intentions, either when he did what he did, or for the future.'

'I'm sure that's right,' said his wife, looking pinch-faced and far from sure. 'In any case, our Prudence would never have gone off with a young man she didn't trust.'

'She didn't have much option,' said Simon.

'Aha!' laughed the collector. 'I hear you swept her off her feet! And perhaps she swept you off yours?'

Simon knew when to keep his own counsel. Throughout lunch (a good one, but not up to Dorcas's standards) he played the country-boy-of-few-words, confining himself to 'aye' and 'này' in as heavy a country burr as he could manage. Prudence's mother, left to herself, would have asked him point-blank, 'Are you going to marry her, and when?' but here, to her extreme annoyance, she was continually frustrated by her husband, who seemed to have lost his wits, and every time she began the question, changed the subject. So caught up were they in this tussle of purposes that only when the meal was nearly over did it occur to them to ask where Prudence was.

'I have left her in the care of some nursing ladies,' said Simon.

'Ah, the Priestesses' Haven of Mercy,' said Prudence's mother. That institution was, in fact, in the very suburb where he had met the collector. She passed on quickly, lest Simon should tell her the Visiting Hours and compel her to visit her daughter. 'Now, just one thing, Simon –'

'More pudding, my dear boy,' said the collector heartily. Then: 'No need for questions, my dear. Simon knows what he's doing.'

When Simon had gone, he said to his wife, who was speechless and shaking with fury, 'Now just you listen to me, because I know what I'm doing too. I've been thinking. If he marries her, well and good, but Prudence will get his worldly goods, and I'm not sure how well she'll serve us if she does. If he doesn't marry her, we'll sue him for all he's got – in her name, of course; but you can leave it to me to see that she doesn't get her hands on it.'

'You think of everything,' said his wife begrudgingly.

'Got to, in my job.'

The superior fiend regretted turning himself into a black beetle. He found himself the prey to nasty predators and very ill received by his own kind, who defended their territory with great hostility. You may wonder why he did not change again into some other form? It is not so easy. Once you have made a decision it makes its claims on you. He was not *much* superior, only a grade higher, in fact, than the wretched spirits already haunting Cankered Wood, and his masters did not intend him to perform his duties comfortably.

He made the most of his lot, leaving the wood to make a reconnaissance of the town, round which (if one may be allowed the term) he wheeled his droning flight. Though he was scarcely noticed, he left his effect. The air was subtly charged with him, and the more sensitive citizens were mysteriously moved. The poet Gabriel, for instance, went off on a sort of hallucinatory trip, which caused him to write one line of singular beauty:

And lousy tinklings drull the distant folds.

He sat enraptured by it. If only he could write the rest

of a poem round it! Then he was seized with doubt. Something wrong somewhere? *Drull*?

The fiend returned to Cankered Wood at nightfall, his wings heavy and with a weight on his mind. His masters would expect results. Confusion was what they were after. This was generally achieved by luring human beings with false hopes, goading them to strive for wrong goals, persuading them to worship wrong gods. But something very disturbing was going on in that witch's hovel, hitherto regarded as a safe constituency; there was an atmosphere, a mood out of keeping with that of Dorcas, who professed to like clubfooted ghouls. The fiend crouched under a leaf and pondered. If things got worse, or, looked at another way, better, there would be harmony.

As he sank deeper into despondency he heard a sound which raised his spirits slightly. It was a plaintive moaning, laced with a high, thin, rare, lugubrious wail. It moved him, as hearing his national anthem might move an exiled patriot.

'It is the crying of the night ones,' he said to himself. 'What music they make.'

And then it occurred to him that those lost souls might be put to use, as rubbish may be recycled to make goods. Was there not an army here, ready to hand? He thrilled to the idea, so that his antennae crackled and he gave off a strong smell of sulphur.

Chapter Thirteen

The thought of Prudence depressed Simon, yet, curiously, touched him too. She was a victim all round. She had been dragged from the hands of a mob and driven into the hands of a witch, and now she must be fetched home. Having met her parents, he believed that this was the worst victimisation of all.

He must return to the hovel and tell her that it was safe for her to go back to the town. But what would she do then?

At any rate, his return must wait till morning. His unwilling lunch with the tax collector had delayed him several hours, and it was now evening, and nothing would induce him to make another journey through the woods at night.

He rose at dawn, saddled Cuthbert, and made a detour through the sleeping suburbs to the brink of Cankered Wood. Passage through the wood by daylight looked easy. It was the night that threw hunch-backed shadows.

Pale sunlight glistened on the gossamer webs on the grass, and filtered through the branches as he entered the wood. At a seemingly short distance, he could see the top of Dorcas's rickety chimney. He dismounted, and then, on an impulse, remounted and looked again in the direction of the hovel. He could no longer see the chimney, even though Cuthbert had not moved from the spot. Frowning, he turned this way and that, trying to prove to himself that he had looked in the wrong direction. He even twisted fully round in the saddle to look behind him to where the field was still visible beyond the edge of the wood. This was stranger still. He could see the sunlight shining on the wet grass, yet it was growing steadily darker in the wood. He turned back, and it was like leaving a lighted room for the dark. He could now see hardly farther than the end of Cuthbert's nose. He twisted round again to look back to the field, but now the field could no longer be seen.

He slipped from Cuthbert's back, clutching the bridle, and could barely distinguish the massive shape of the horse from the solid darkness. He stretched out his left arm and could not see the hand at the end of it. He wondered whether he was going blind.

The sounds began.

Simon was not a prey to imaginative fears, but a shiver had gone through him when Prudence had said, in that direful voice of hers, *It is the crying of the night ones*. This was what he heard now; the same dejected moaning; but very faint and far away. It grew stronger, and now it was not only mournful, but menacing.

Shapes began forming.

So he was not going blind. Through the trees, in half a dozen places, he saw grey blobs like small drifting clouds. They were closing in on him. As they loomed up behind the trees he saw that each blob had a human face.

It was as if the severed heads of corpses were hanging in the air. Their voices were stronger now, not moaning but jeering. Cuthbert stamped and broke into a terrified whinny. Like an echo, the horrible faces took this up, and a cackling mockery of Cuthbert's whinny repeated itself through the trees.

Simon's powerful muscles were no use against this. He wished he had paid attention when Sophie was talking to Dorcas, but it had had no meaning for him. Certain phrases, however, did stick in his mind. 'Mind over matter! All in the mind! You are haunted only by your own fears!'

Strange talk. Nevertheless he bunched his muscles, drew a deep breath, and shouted, 'I'm not afraid of you! You needn't think I am! You don't exist!'

The faces, which had been sick with evil like melting wax, all broke into twisted grins; and then the woods resounded with their raucous and unearthly laughter.

In the town the day was fair enough. And yet the nerves and emotions of the townsfolk were disturbed, without their knowing why. The ringleaders of the mob that had attacked Prudence were particularly disturbed. They grew passionately remorseful, and began making speeches in the town square, declaring that they had tried to burn a saint. Pretty soon their old mob had formed again, and took up their protestations with cries and lamentations and much shedding of tears. What must they do now but swarm to the tax collector's house, with the object of begging him to bring back his holy daughter with all possible speed, so that they might escort her to a temple and hold a great service in her honour.

The tax collector and his wife were having breakfast. The workmen who were practically rebuilding their house had not yet turned up. They had last been working on the roof, and had left it propped up on posts. The mob pounded through the collector's garden and poured into his house through the unlocked back door. They were shouting, 'Noble sir, bring us back your saintly daughter, that we may honour her' (Urstwileans in times of emotional stress had a turn for rhetoric) but the precise nature of their request was lost in the uproar, and the collector and his wife assumed that they were on the rampage again. They fled upstairs, with the mob leaping after them with beseeching cries. Several members of it collided with the props and knocked them out of position, and the roof fell in, causing a number of nasty bumps and bruises, and killing the collector and his wife stone dead. If they had not dishonestly claimed a new roof from the state, this could not have happened.

Bleep, bleep.

'Sophie? Sophie, the Urstwile graph is showing violent oscillations.'

'Probably something it ate.'

'Do be serious. There seems to be a grave imbalance, and with the elections so near there could be *disastrous* consequences.'

'Don't blame me. I haven't been out of doors for two days.'

'But you may be able to help. The Commissioners are most anxious to get to the cause of this. If you notice anything untoward, you are to report it immediately.'

'All right.'

'*Discreetly*, Sophie.'

'All right.'

Before Simon reached the wood that morning, Dorcas had set off on her broomstick to the regions of the Urstwilean nobility, to see if they had left any little luxuries out for her. They made a practice of doing this, in the way that people in folk tales left presents for the elves.

'Elevation,' she murmured to herself, relishing her new knowledge. 'Mind-over-matter. Science.' But the broomstick stalled a couple of times, and only when she muttered one of her old incantations did she make it rise at all. But Sophie had told her, *any* words will do so long as you believe in them, so she was still being scientific and all was well. Soon she was flying over the trees in sunlight that still filtered through them to the earth.

Sophie was left alone with Prudence. Prudence was exasperating her and worrying her. The girl would not eat. She lay pale and silent, and quite beautiful in a frail, delicate way, because her face was no longer clenched into the old priggish expression, but relaxed and re-signed, and her eyes had become very large, and held so strange a light that Sophie could hardly bear to look at them. Prudence had evidently made up her mind that Sophie was not preparing her for a sacrifice, after all. Her face, calm and defeated, made Sophie uneasy. She remembered how, when they were having breakfast with Dorcas, the girl had looked at Simon's face, at the same time that he was gazing so adoringly at her own, and had looked away again in pain, and then, a moment afterwards, had fainted. There lay the clue to Prudence's illness, and to the look she was directing at Sophie now.

Even so . . . Sophie scowled and went downstairs.

'Why should I be sorry for you?' she muttered. 'I'm not giving in to you that easily. I'll look after you till you're well and that'll be the end of it. When Simon tells us it's safe again we'll send you back home.'

Home. Pretty surely the worst place to send her to.

Sympathy crept in again. Prudence was being obsti-nate and very brave. By the extraordinary standards of Urstwile, she could have insisted that Simon should behave 'honourably' and marry her, but she hadn't; nor would she allow him to discuss the matter. No claims, no word of reproach. It was out of character, somehow. It was disarming.

She stamped angrily back upstairs. 'Look,' she said harshly, 'he's yours if you want him. Stop being a martyr, will you. Tell him so.'

Prudence rolled her large eyes towards Sophie without moving her head, rather in the manner of her mother, but with an expression in them that her mother's would never have held. 'If that's what you think,' it said, 'you don't begin to understand.' Sophie flushed and needlessly plumped up Prudence's pillows.

'Never mind, forget it.'

She went downstairs, slowly, heavy at heart. The light seemed to be fading in sympathy with her mood. It was never very light in the hovel, because of the windows, which Dorcas was obliged to leave filthy, but now it was as if night were coming on. She went to the door and looked out. As she did so, all went black, ebony black.

Ebony reminded her of the new name she wanted Simon to give Cuthbert. And now, not far off, she heard Cuthbert neigh, right on cue. His voice was high-pitched and full of terror. A moment later, a jeering parody of his neighing echoed all over the wood. She heard Simon's voice, shouting, defiant. This was unnerving. He was afraid.

And then laughter. It was the cruellest, coarsest, most hateful laughter ever heard. The woods were sick with it.

'Simon!' she called, 'Simon, Simon!' She was badly shaken. There were forces here that her science could not explain.

There were gleams in the blackness and she saw

Simon, and Cuthbert too, so near that they were within the clearing where the hovel stood. Man and horse stood still like stone. Between them and the hovel drifted a barrage of dreadful disconnected faces. They crept nearer. Sophie sprang back and slammed the door.

Chapter Fourteen

The slightly superior fiend was experimenting rather than following a settled plan. Using malevolent magic, he had yoked the lost souls of Cankered Wood to the gang of yobbo demons he had been sent here to discipline, and the result was a flotilla of gibbous balloons with dyspeptic faces that uttered uncouth laughter. Neither he nor they had any clear idea what they were doing. They enjoyed frightening Simon and the horse, but they were not mainly concerned with them. Their general drift was towards the hovel, where, as the fiend had already discovered, a strange force was at work, something gentle and suffering yet very strong, and dangerous to their cause.

Whatever it was, the only way of defeating it was to make it lose faith in itself. When faith is lost, all is lost. The fiend, still reluctantly encased in the body of a black beetle, flew and crawled by turns to the door of the hovel. His army, like very black sheep, followed him. He had just settled on the leg of a ferret, dangling in the porch, when the door opened and a young girl looked out. He had seen her before. Possibly she was the source of the power within, possibly not. In any case, the place for him was inside, observing the fifth column; and so for the second time the fiend slipped unobserved into the hovel, and hid himself in the grate.

Dorcas had a stroke of luck as soon as she set foot in the lands of the gentry. She was summoned by the princess Marionetta, who had no idea of the value of money and gave costly gifts regardless. The princess dwelt in a turret at the top of a white castle which looked like a huge magnification of Reuben's tooth. She spent most of her time murmuring 'He cometh not', and declaring that she was aweary, aweary, and wished that she were dead. The rest of the time she spent looking through a gigantic telescope, a family heirloom constructed by an ancestor who had been persecuted for saying that the earth moved round the sun, but which the princess used for spying on the townsfolk in order to deplore their morals. She always asked Dorcas the same question: 'Tell me, when shall my true love come?', but would have been most put out had any man really put in an appearance. She was a comely woman, running a bit to fat for want of exercise, with long yellow plaits which she sometimes hung out of the window.

'Tell me, you knowledgeable crone,' she said to Dorcas, 'when shall my true love come? And how shall I lure him hither? Speak.'

Questions of this kind were easy for Dorcas. 'You must obtain a sprig of the plant *Canis odoriferus*, your highness, and plant it in earth dug from the footprints of a nightingale till it flowers, and then sleep with the cut flowers beneath your pillow for seven nights.'

'I shall despatch a menial for the required items. *Canis . . .?*'

'*Odoriferus*, your highness. In common speech it is called *Dogsbreath*.'

'I eschew common speech,' said the princess austerely, 'but, indeed, the term might come more easily to the lips of a scullion. *Dogsbreath*.'

Every gardener knows that Dogsbreath will grow only in a compound of powdered glass and iron filings, but this did not matter, as the princess would never get round to obtaining any. With a sigh of, 'Ah, how heavily hang the hollyhocks!' she put an eye to the telescope, and then recoiled as if it had stung her.

'Something is going on down there,' she said in a voice faint with distaste. 'Some of the rabble appear to have sustained an injury. You will watch for me. I am very sensitive, and cannot bear the suffering of others.'

Dorcas looked through the splendid telescope and found that it was focused directly on to the house of the tax collector, which was a pile of débris with clouds of dust issuing from it, and from which some feverishly working rescuers had uncovered a pair of mangled corpses. The sight fired her interest, but she merely reported, 'The house of a couple of citizens has fallen down, your highness.'

'Poor wretches,' said the princess languidly, 'why cannot they live in properly built castles, as we do?' She turned to the window. 'O life, thou long disease,' she sighed, 'when shall I be rid of thee?'

Flying back with gifts of more rare herbs and a jewel-encrusted snuff-box, Dorcas ran into fog as she entered Cankered Wood from the west side, and had to make a forced landing. Only, of course, it was not fog. At first she thought that the hell-broth had boiled dry and was burning. Her next thought was that Sophie might have been tampering with magic spells in her absence, like the sorcerer's apprentice, but that was unlikely too, as Sophie had spells enough of her own. Her third thought was that the elementals who had gone on the spree on the night of the Chief Elder's visit were on the warpath again and were making a mass attack. This thought was her decisive one; and mumbling protective spells to herself, with all notions of science and psychology gone from her head, Dorcas began walking towards her home, holding her broomstick like a gun.

A tree got in her way. She gave it a quick glare of her yellow eyes and it sprang into place and kept still, like a fidgetting soldier on parade who catches the sergeant's eye. But there was dread in her heart.

It quickly became known in the town that 'accidental death' would be the verdict on the tax collector and his wife, and the citizens forgot all about remorse and flocked to the inns and kissed one another and bought one another drinks. The poet Gabriel, who had lately become cynical, looked sourly on at them, and wrote the following epigram:

> *Fools! no sooner shall they hearse one*
> *Than they shall endure a worse one.*

But then some warm-hearted neighbours spotted him through his window and dragged him from his house and haled him to an inn and bought him drinks in which he drowned his cynicism until he had to be helped back home. 'When shall we three meet again?' he asked his reflection in the mirror.

Meanwhile some of the young men were bold enough to reel down the high street bawling snatches from another poem, the one about the ash-blonde witch.

Reprehensible though this was, no-one tried to stop them, and a spirit of carnival prevailed all day. And all this disturbance was caused by the presence of a measly little fiend in the shape of a black beetle in a wood miles away! The greatest consequences may spring from the smallest causes.

Nor were the effects limited to Urstwile. In Sophie's

country itself, the Urstwile graph was having con-
vulsions. 'Imbalance' was obvious, and this in its
mysterious way affected the population's emotions and
loyalties. The pre-election opinion polls, which were
compiled by electronic thought-reading and were deadly
accurate, were showing a dramatic swing in favour of
the Neo-Radicals:

Neo-Radicals 96%
Party in the Right 1%
Don't Know 3%

Revolution was nigh. Meanwhile, in Dorcas's hovel,
the black beetle bumbled about behind his log.

Sophie, having slammed the door, paused for a
moment, then ran upstairs to Prudence. The fiend
watched her, puzzled, but with the excited inkling of
an idea that this was the one to watch. 'Simon, Simon!'
she had called. She was in love, and where there is love
there is always a chance of devilry. He hopefully awaited
Simon's arrival.

'Why is it dark?' demanded Prudence in a feeble
voice, as Sophie lit the oil lamp.

'Eclipse of the sun.'

'Who was at the door?'

'No-one. Lie down.'

'It's dark because of me.'

'Do you think you're so important that the sun goes
out for you?'

'They've come for me.'

'Who have?'

'The evil ones.'

Rather egoistical to take it so personally, thought

Sophie, but Prudence was probably, and disturbingly, right about their visitors. But she replied severely:

'Don't talk nonsense. Whatever awful crime do you think you've committed?'

Prudence lay back and did not answer. She had no words for what she felt. She had, of course, committed the very sin she had so sternly condemned in others, but she could readily have forgiven herself for that if Simon had loved her. As it was, he did not. He was in love with this other fatal woman, and because of that Prudence had no wish to live.

The greatest thrill of her life had been when Simon had snatched her from the mob and carried her away on his horse. It had been wonderful; it had been an oft-dreamed daydream come true; it had made being half-lynched worth while. But it had been immediately followed by humiliation: Simon had rescued the wrong girl, and plainly couldn't stand the sight of her. Prudence drew no hope from their night together. She had been conveniently female, that was all.

His attempts afterwards to do the decent thing had humiliated her even more. The final blow had been to encounter the ash-blonde witch in all her beauty, and to see how hopelessly infatuated Simon was with her. Prudence wished to exact no obligations from him. Her father spent his life exacting obligations, and was hated for it. She didn't want to live to be hated. Hell itself, rather than hell on earth.

Simon, as the cruel laughter died and the faces turned away from him, unstuck himself from the spot and began trudging towards the hovel. His desire to run in the opposite direction almost overpowered him, but he mastered it. He clung to Cuthbert's bridle, and Cuthbert, having no-one to cling to, champed his bit.

Having survived the first shock, Simon felt more at ease. He even managed to tell himself, as the odious faces stopped laughing and veered away, that only children and weaklings were scared of ugly faces, and that anyway these were not looking primarily for him. He did not wholly convince himself on either point, but he kept on towards the hovel, for which they seemed to be bound. They served as lanterns; he could see the hovel, dimly, in their bilious light.

He saw the door of the hovel open, and Sophie standing in the doorway. For a shocked moment he thought that she was opening the door *to* them. But she slammed it shut, and he went on.

For whom did he go on? For Prudence. Nor was it just a matter of duty. Slyly, like the slow advance of a disease, Prudence was getting under his skin. Ever since he had tried to make her an honourable offer and she had refused to listen, she had somehow *mattered* to him. She had done so even more since he had met her parents. This feeling for her, like rising damp, was even beginning to quench his ardour for Sophie. He felt worried about his own constancy. In guilt and doubt, he went on.

Suddenly he saw Dorcas, who had herself just seen the floating faces, and was advancing warily, as if through a field of mines. He was more pleased to see the witch than he would ever have thought possible. He hurried to her like a child to its mother.

'What are they?' he asked.

Dorcas, who for as long as she could remember hadn't liked seeing anyone much, felt a positively maternal pang of sympathy for him.

'They are bad dreams.' Then she caught herself up and became tough and practical. 'You've come back for Prudence? There's news for her. Her parents are dead.'

'Dead!'

'Yes. Will you commiserate with her or congratulate her?'

'How did they die?' Simon had gone pale. What a load of responsibility now fell on him!

'Their house fell down and they forgot to duck.'

Dazed, he followed her towards the hovel. Even during this exchange of words, something had happened. It had grown lighter, and the hideous faces had clustered aimlessly round the far end of the hovel as boats will drift together in a bay. Even their faces were less facial than before. They seemed to be losing definition. They now looked more like the rough resemblances of faces accidentally formed by clouds or patterns in carpets. There was less concentrated venom in the air. The glass was rising.

Sophie greeted Simon much less effusively than on the previous occasion.

'You left us just in time,' she said coldly and most unreasonably. 'Missed all the fun, haven't you?'

'I have a message for Prudence,' he replied soberly. 'It's safe for her to go back to the town now. But her parents are dead.'

'Dead?'

Dorcas explained what she had seen through Marionetta's telescope.

'I see,' said Sophie, and indeed she saw all that this meant. Desert the kid now? 'Well,' she said to Simon, becoming suddenly pitiful, 'I hope you haven't left it too late.'

She led him upstairs, while Dorcas sat by the hearth and looked quizzically and sadly at the cat, who by now had stopped bristling at the presence of demons and was dozing indifferently in the grate. Prudence lay on her mattress with her eyes closed and a waxen calm on her face. Simon caught his breath.

'Is she very ill?'

'She's dying.'

'But how has this happened? Did she catch a fever that night in the wood?'

'I think she's dying for you,' said Sophie.

He was silent for a very long time. Sophie watched his face and understood its look. He felt needed. He felt indispensable. Even against his will, he was bound to this girl. Later he would realise, reluctantly perhaps, even with a sort of dismay, that what he felt was love.

She looked at Prudence with amazement. Who would have guessed she had it in her? Of course, anyone who ticks off courting couples in the act of courting, and challenges a powerful witch with her own weapons, must have plenty of nerve; but whoever would have thought there was so much love in her? It was like discovering a new chemical element. That element had made Prudence a winner against all odds.

She said to Simon, 'You know what to do.'

'You knew, didn't you?' he whispered. 'You brought this about.'

'Did I?' said Sophie enigmatically. 'Then don't waste time.'

She walked away downstairs. Simon slipped his big hands under Prudence's shoulders and raised her waxen cheek to his own.

'Come on, lass,' he said, kissing the sleeping beauty, 'I'm taking you home. Our home.'

Chapter Fifteen

The oafish demons had lost concentration for no deeper reason than that they were bored. It had been fun at first, to be joined to the lost souls of the wood, and pull faces, and make noises, but they lacked application, and lost interest, and began to fall apart. The fiend, ensconced behind the log in the grate, sensed this feeling but was unable to do anything about it. Like the Urstwile spy who posed as a scarecrow, he had put himself into a position from where he could do nothing but fume.

And now the truth dawned on him. It was so frightful that, as far as a black beetle can manage it, he turned white. There was the deadliest spirit of all inside this hovel. There was love.

He could have kicked himself, which, again, is hard for a beetle. He had sensed the presence of love all right, but he had picked the wrong kind and matched the wrong pair. He had had Sophie and Simon in mind. There lay infatuation and the romantic boloney. Fiends can make plenty of mischief out of that. But, just as in a detective story where the least likely suspect turns out to be the murderer, it was in Prudence, the little prig who lay quietly expiring upstairs, that true love was to be found. If only he had realised it soon enough, he might have brought his powers to bear sufficiently to make her die of grief in good time, or at least despair and drag out from day to day a living death. But the blonde witch had got her speech in first, and had foiled him. And now true love prevailed. It is a force no fiend can defeat.

In panic he ran out from behind the log and scuttled across the hearth, at which the cat, who had no moral sense at all but simply pounced on anything that moved, awoke from sleep and pinned him down with a quick dab of her paw. She released him, let him run two inches, then pinned him down again.

Sophie had just come into the room, saturated with pity for herself for the sacrifice she had just made. The sight of the cat toying with the beetle swept her into a fierce and sudden change of mood. With a flash of insight she understood what the cat had caught; Prudence's 'monster with a horrible face' took on a meaning for her.

On Dorcas's sideboard was a mahogany case of great value, containing two glass bottles. Sophie took one of these, removed the broad stopper, and crept towards the cat on hands and knees. The cat hissed with a hellish open mouth, but Dorcas, who was still wearing her spiteful boots, drove it back with a quick pass of her foot, and Sophie clapped the bottle over the beetle before it had time to run.

Then she inverted the bottle with a swift jerk, and as the beetle fell to the bottom, triumphantly replaced the stopper. It had a screwtop, beautifully made. It locked tight.

The beetle was changing from black to red. Its crimson glow suffused the glass. Little horns appeared, and a tail. Tiny sparks of sulphurous light flashed from its eyes. It was in a tremendous tantrum, and exceedingly nasty, and futile, and absurd.

'Small fry, this,' said Dorcas contemptuously. 'But these things are terrible disease carriers.'

'Like rats?'

'Worse than rats.'

She put the bottle back in the mahogany case and locked the lid with a key. 'In the grounds of the Baron Dunfor's castle,' she remarked, 'there is a bottomless well. I'm going to throw this down it. A pity, it looked nice on the sideboard. I must visit her Highness Marionetta again and try to get a replacement.'

She gave Sophie a puzzled, admiring look. 'You were quick,' she said. 'Caught on in a flash, didn't you? But you're not going to tell me *that* – ' she prodded the mahogany case – 'is just a product of our imagination, are you?'

'Oh no,' said Sophie, with a shudder.

'I can't make you out,' said Dorcas. 'You know so much, and so little. Are you really one of us? Or what are you?'

'I wish I knew, Dorcas. I'm beginning to think that my people back home have got it all wrong.'

Prudence was convalescing. Sitting up in bed, starry-eyed, pink-cheeked, and with her lips slightly parted in bliss and wonder, she really looked very pretty. Simon hovered over her like a devoted husband awaiting the birth of his first child, which part he would probably play in earnest in the course of months. Sophie could not help feeling a passing wish to kick her, but perhaps not very hard.

'I've made a proper mess of everything, though,' she said to herself. 'Why did I have to interfere with the little twit in the first place? Why couldn't I leave well alone?'

Prudence would be happier as a wife than a priestess,

perhaps. But what about Dorcas? Surely she would lose credibility as a witch now? How could she pretend to be bad when the awful news got round that she was good? She might as well be someone's grandmother.

And what about Sophie herself? What fearful retribution would fall on her when she told them the truth back home?

But all the same, she had to tell them, if only to force them to recall her. She *had* to get out of Urstwile, whatever the cost. The presence of Simon, dotingly bestowing his love on another girl, was more than she could bear.

So far, her father had done all the bleeping, picking his own times, when he was sure of not being overheard. If she bleeped him it might catch him at an awkward moment.

'If I wait a while he'll be at the university,' she thought. 'It'll be safe to speak to him there.'

'Sophie –' said the professor apprehensively.

'You told me to report anything important. Well, this is very important. I think we've got it all wrong back home. You see –'

'*Be careful what you are saying.*'

'No, I'm sick of being careful. Listen. I've always been taught to believe in scientific truth. Fine. Well, the scientific truth is that superstitions are true. Well, I mean, not all of them, walking under ladders and that sort of thing, but some of them are. I'm living with a real witch and I've just caught a real devil. Horrid little thing. But he's not just something in the mind. As a matter of fact, he's in a bottle –'

'Sophie,' said the professor in agony, 'this is election day.'

'Is it? Well, may the best man win. Dad, listen. There

is such a thing as love. It's *not* just "a psychological aura arising out of an exact balance of hormones". It's real, like electricity –'

'Oh my *God!*' groaned the professor.

'As for that,' said Sophie, 'I think there is One. God, I mean.'

There followed a hoarse rustling like atmospherics, which was the professor struggling for breath.

'Sophie,' he choked at last, 'the university is a polling station, and all incoming calls are being monitored.'

'Oh,' said Sophie.

Then her spirit revolted. 'Well,' she said, 'will they mind monitoring the truth? Or is it more than they can face?'

Simon, who liked to get things straight, had now made up his mind about Sophie. She came from heaven. She was his guardian angel. That explained her innocence, her purity, her unearthly beauty and her miraculous powers of healing. Also her flying. An angel. A flying one . . .

His belief was reinforced when the robot called to take her away. It was an awe-inspiring sight. A ball of light appeared above the clearing in which the hovel stood. It glowed with a soft, peachy radiance. (This was an innovation of its engineers, who had caused its light to be heavily diffused, in case it injured the sight of those watching it.) It sank to the ground, bounced gently like a balloon, and then became a crystalline sphere of such limpid beauty that even Dorcas, who was sceptical about all visual display, including sunsets, could only gasp with admiration, while Simon and Prudence, trembling in the doorway of the hovel, sank to their knees in awe.

A curved panel in the side of the sphere opened, and

a being stepped out whom Simon took to be a heavenly messenger, but who was in fact a strikingly handsome robot, all in white. Simon was a little disappointed that he had no wings. Or perhaps, after all, he had some, fitted flush into his back, in the way that the door was in the sphere. He spoke courteously in a beautifully modulated voice.

'Orders are to return at once, Miss.'

'I was expecting them,' said Sophie.

A last, parting hug for Simon? She turned, and found him and Prudence on their knees, covering their faces with their hands, and peering at the marvel from between their fingers. No, he was on the same plane as Prudence, and she herself was from another world, and to entice him again, even for a moment, even with the sanction of saying goodbye, just wouldn't be fair. They both looked up at her, worshipfully, and so she did what seemed most appropriate, even though she felt idiotic doing it: she laid a hand on each of their heads.

'Bless you, my children,'

She turned to Dorcas. The witch had put on her full regalia, pointed hat, spiteful boots, emblematic gown and all. She was wearing her most malevolent expression. None of this disguised the fact that she was near tears.

'Oh, *Dorcas*,' said Sophie.

'Don't worry about me,' said Dorcas, in her harshest croak. 'Good riddance to the lot of you. I'm sick of you all. The sooner I get back to cursing people the better.'

But she looked like one of the ugly sisters watching Cinderella drive off, a smug little victor, in the stage coach. Simon's face softened. He sympathised with nasty people.

Sophie spotted the look in his eyes from between his fingers. 'Remember, Simon,' she said. 'Don't you neglect her. She's been good to you.'

Her word was law now. He bowed his head in acquiescence.

'Promise.'

He nodded reverently.

She was going to add, 'And be good to Prudence, too,' but a lump rose in her throat and thwarted her. She took Dorcas in her arms and hugged her.

'I'll never, never forget you.'

'Huh!' said Dorcas, and sniffed viciously, and wiped her nose with the back of her hand.

The robot intervened. 'Orders are to return, Miss.'

'I'm saying goodbye to my friends.'

'The best of friends must part,' said the robot, 'but absence makes the heart grow fonder.'

'Yes,' said Sophie, 'and the angles at the base of an isosceles triangle are equal, and Marmite is a vegetable product, and a Boy Scout is kind to animals. Come on, I'm ready.'

The sphere rose like an iridescent bubble, and then, like a bubble, vanished. Within seconds Sophie could look back at the great mountain ridge that separated Urstwile from the world. So ultimate a barrier did it seem that it was hard to believe that life existed beyond it. Yet she could still feel that she was leaving a real world behind, and returning to a fake and sterile one.

'Stirred them up a bit, though, didn't I?' she said to herself, and grinned. And no sooner did she grin than she thought her heart would break.

Sophie was much missed in Urstwile, not least by the horse Cuthbert. He had so much wanted to be renamed Ebony. But she was gone, and no-one else would think of it now.

Chapter Sixteen

The Neo-Radicals had won by a huge number of votes. There were new faces everywhere, some of the street names were changed, and a new currency was introduced. Sophie had little idea what it all meant, save a very vague one that the country was ruined. She wondered whether this new government would restore capital punishment and hang her, or whether she would get away with life imprisonment. Her father had disappeared, she supposed into exile. When she was told that he had gone off to some northern university to receive an honorary doctorate, she suspected that this was a plot to lure him to his death.

But gradually it came home to her that she was popular and admired. What the old government would have condemned as anti-social, the new one applauded as public-spirited. She was summoned to appear before the new High Commissioner. He was an enormous man with a booming voice which sounded as if he were shouting in his bath. He asked her permission to call her Miss Oakroyd, because, he said, his government was anxious to restore the polite formalities.

'Having been away from the country for a while, Miss Oakroyd, you may not be quite clear as to what our policies are.'

'No,' said Sophie, and then, remembering the polite formalities, added 'sir'.

The High Commissioner looked over her head and launched into reverberating speech. The new government, he said, would get away from sterile intellectuality and scientific claptrap. They would re-explore the regions of myth and legend, the subculture of folklore, the twilight world of fantasy and fairy tale. They were especially interested in the Conservation of Urstwile. They believed that they could learn much from those wise and simple people.

'In your last communication, Miss Oakroyd, you mentioned a witch . . .'

Sophie, who had been losing track, sat up and said, 'Yes? – er – sir?'

'Is she in your opinion an authentic one?'

'Oh yes. She's up to her ears in myth and legend, the subculture of folklore, and the twilight world of fantasy and fairytale.'

'You do put it well,' said the High Commissioner, marvelling.

'She's a super cook, too.'

'Ah, back to nature, back to nature,' sighed the High Commissioner. 'Such a person could teach us to live again. Do you think she would consent to come here as a resident consultant?'

Sophie gulped.

'You are thinking,' said the High Commissioner anxiously, 'that she might not be willing to leave her Arcadian paradise for this place?'

Sophie's heart was racing. Dorcas was a misfit in Urstwile, and this could be a bigger break than she'd ever dreamed of. But she had sense enough to seem to weigh the question.

'Well . . .'

'Do you think she might be persuaded?'

'She might, if you paid her enough.'

It was nearly a year, however, before Sophie was sent to Urstwile again. In their ardour to be natural and spontaneous, the new government set up a series of committees which went on so long that Sophie feared that the old government might get back in before they'd done anything. After some months, however, they began sending robot spies (disguised as dustmen, scarecrows, etc.,) to sound out the land. The spies did this by planting metal bugs in strategic places. These were the size of a fingernail, and disturbingly like the blackbeetle-fiend Sophie had caught in the hovel. They could not only record the speech of the Urstwileans but could also make comments on it, and were a great advance on the old electronic graph.

Sophie ordered the robot pilot to land the sphere at the edge of Cankered Wood, resolving to make the rest of the journey by personal flight. Birchbrooms were unobtainable at home, so she had brought along a small vacuum cleaner, which she now straddled with some misgiving. But her college lecturer had been right: any kind of pole would aid levitation if you put your mind to it; and soon she was sailing blithely over the trees, which chattered among their leaves in disgust, having no means of obstructing her.

Dorcas, in full uniform, was stirring the hell-broth and singing morosely to herself:

> *I rather like bugs and beetles*
> *And lice and household flies,*
> * And worms that creep*
> * Six feet deep*
> *Through the sockets of dead men's eyes;*
> *I rather like rigor mortis –*

But before she could find another rhyme for 'much', which would have set her quite a problem, Sophie alighted in the clearing. The witch stopped singing and her eyes lit up like golden candles, and without ado she hustled her indoors and served her with a beverage made from rare herbs.

She listened to Sophie's proposals and, unconsciously completing her rhyme in her head, she said, 'That would give me pleasure beyond all measure. I'd like that ever so much. But how long would it last?'

'All your life.'

'But suppose you had another change of government?'

'They wouldn't sack you. The worst they'd do would be to make you a lecturer in levitation, but my guess is that you'd soon be as much in league with our commissioners as you are with your Elders here.'

'I wouldn't like to leave my treasures.'

'We'll take them with us.'

'Where would I live?'

'In a castle. They're building one for you.'

'With a turret?'

'Yes, of course, dear. With a *lovely* turret.'

'You can do everything,' said Dorcas wonderingly.

Then she added sadly, 'Except give me back my youth.'

'Well, as for that,' said Sophie, 'we can go quite a long way. You're not really old, Dorcas, you only think you are. There are people in my country older than you who look about thirty. Remedial exercise, you know. Straighten your back. Restore your figure. And teeth, of course. New teeth. They'd do wonders for your face.'

'You could give me new *teeth*?'

'Yes, and these wouldn't ache.'

Sophie had had the foresight to bring a robot dentist with her, one of the best in the country, with a string of qualifications and a nice line in amiable chatter. She now summoned the sphere to the clearing and he got to work. Dentistry in the Twenty-second Century was not only painless but a positive pleasure, and almost instantaneous, so that in a few minutes Dorcas's sprinkling of yellow spikes was extracted and she was equipped with a full set of beautiful white teeth, which separated her nose from her chin and gave her face a noble acquiline look. While she was under hypnosis another robot doctor, a psycho-therapist, suggested to her that her hair was not grey and wispy but luxuriant and dark, so that it began rapidly to thicken and turn black, in much the same way, in reverse, that the hair of the poor lost travellers of the wood had turned white overnight. She changed from her witch's regalia to a magnificent golden gown, and looked so regal and splendid that Sophie feared for a moment that the Commissioners might be disappointed, expecting someone more witch-like. But no: although they were nuts about Nature, they would prefer it pretty.

The sphere was of unlimited elasticity, and could have shipped a cathedral had it needed to, and in no time all Dorcas's valuables were loaded into it, leaving only the outer shell of the hovel, with the dried animals dangling dismally in the porch and the hell-broth seething sluggishly, its scum looking like the surface of a dying planet. The cat, who hated travelling, set up a mournful yawp as they set off, but she had only just finished saying 'mi', and had barely reached 'ow', when the sphere landed again. Sophie had ordered it down in the field where Simon's farmhouse stood.

'You are making a mistake, sister.'

'I am their fairy godmother,' said Sophie.

'You should let robots do that sort of thing for you.'

134

'One last goodbye?'

'You'll regret it.'

'Our new government is introducing marriage,' said Sophie. 'It's very popular. Thousands of couples have rushed to sign on. If I'd known they were going to do that . . .'

'You'd have married too, and lived happily ever after?'

Sophie sighed. 'No', she said.

Prudence hoisted her baby up to her face and said, 'Oo's a sweetie-weetie-weetie den? Oo's a boofle, boofle, boofle, boofle, boofle-woofle *boy*??!!' The baby stared back at her with a face like a clenched fist, and the bug planted just outside the window recorded: '*Mother to infant*: language excessively tautological, expressive of spontaneous overflow of instinctive affection rather than considered assessment of infant's merits.'

Simon came in and tickled the baby under the chin.

'Oh look!' exclaimed Prudence. 'He's watching the light as it catches your ring! See? See his eyes?'

'So he is.' Simon twisted the ring this way and that before the baby, who remained as inscrutable as a face on a totem pole. 'He's going to be intelligent, I reckon.'

'Oh yes, look what a high forehead he's got!' And so he had; as he was quite bald, his forehead stretched to the back of his neck.

'He's *boofle*!!' said Prudence.

Sophie, sitting on a bench in the sun just outside the house, heard all this with mixed feelings. Nothing against the kid, but perhaps Dorcas was right, perhaps this visit had been a mistake. Not that they had been badly received; ceremoniously, indeed, as befits fairy godmothers. Prudence had brought out the best china (it was a wedding present from Dorcas and was priceless) and had racked her brain to give them fine meals. But, hospitable though they were, there was an air of condescension about them which nettled Sophie a bit. In producing this baby they had done something unique in history, and they lived in a circle from which the rest of the world, however goodnaturedly, was shut out. Their greatest compliment to Sophie was to give her the baby to hold. She would hold it gingerly away from her with much the same grip as she would have given a cocktail shaker. Her awkwardness amused them. They admired her, they held her in awe, but all the same they had something which she lacked, and she suspected that they had an affectionate laugh at her when they were alone.

Prudence's figure had filled out; she was comely like a young matron, and she looked at the world with eyes calm with happiness. Simon's pleasant drawl was more genial than ever. It is not easy to share the joy of people who have no need of you. For although Sophie might still be a guardian angel, she was a superannuated one.

'Would you like to hold him?' said Prudence.

'Come here, poppet,' said Sophie, and apprehensively took hold of the skinny bundle, who was wearing long clothes and looked like an elongated tadpole.

'See how he looks at you? He knows you now! I'm sure he does!'

Prudence went indoors for a few moments. Dorcas said, 'Are you enjoying yourself?'

'Not altogether. He smells of milk and sick.'

'Give him here.' Dorcas took the baby and held him in an expert fashion over her shoulder. 'In ten years' time,' she said, 'there will be nine more like him. Have you thought of that?'

'So I had a narrow escape?'

Dorcas grinned, showing the splendid new teeth. 'Oh yes,' she said. 'And so did Simon.'

Prudence drew Sophie aside as she was walking to the sphere.

'Sophie, I've never thanked you properly for all you've done. You've been wonderful. Simon and I both think you're wonderful. You know that, don't you?'

'I owe a bit to you, too.'

'Sophie, are you really an angel? Or a witch? Or what are you?'

'A bit of both, darling. We all are. Mind how you use it.'

Simon tried to bow as Sophie and Dorcas got into the sphere, but he was holding the baby, and recovered himself, rather as if he were fumbling a catch. He held it up and made it wave its hand. Sophie, waving back, was touched. 'Certainly not ten,' she said to herself, 'nor five either, but one, maybe? I might settle for one.'

'You are sad,' said Dorcas.

'No.'

'I was afraid you would be.'

The robot pilot turned his head. 'Into each life,' he remarked, 'a little rain must fall, but it is an ill wind that blows no-one any good.'

The sphere rose skyward.

'*Dorcas*!' exclaimed Sophie severely.

In her new role as Assistant Oracle, she was helping Dorcas to unpack, or rather, she was doing all the unpacking unaided, for Dorcas, the Oracle herself, was wandering round in a dream, testing the doors that opened when she approached, the lights that went on when she waved her hand, and the lift that rose like a thermometer to the turret in the stars. She had been given a castle, on the edge of the State University campus, that made the Princess Marionetta's look like a dog kennel.

'I thought,' said Sophie, holding up a mahogany case, 'that you were going to throw this down a bottom-less well?'

'I couldn't bear to part with it,' said Dorcas apologetically.

'But is the Thing still inside?'

'It's only a little one.'

'Suppose it gets out?'

'I'll throw it away tomorrow,' said Dorcas humbly.

Music came faintly to their ears. Sophie opened a window and saw a group of students on the grass below. One was playing a guitar, and all were singing a pop song which had come from nowhere out of the ether and was currently taking the country by storm. Their voices were flutey and meek, yet peculiarly charged with subversive menace.

> . . . *murderous, murderous,*
> *The great red roses . . .*

Sophie closed the window. 'No, don't bother,' she said. 'Even if it does get out, I don't suppose it'll make much difference.'